T

Elizabeth Rowan Keith

DEDICATION

David H. Keith

a love of many lifetimes

The Lie

My son was born between two young women who wished they knew more about what they were doing. He came as the howls of labor mingled with the roars and shrieks of an early spring blizzard. As the storm quieted, we listened to his first cries.

That's when the lie began. At first, I didn't know about it. Later the lie became mine.

I was a war bride. I was 17. He was 21. My husband and I met at a canteen near the Carolina coast. He was on his way home for leave. It was love at first sight. He stepped through the door and looked around only as far as our eyes met. Later he said it was as if I had been sent there to wait for him.

I thought I was there to serve sandwiches, but I wasn't going to argue.

We spent every day and evening together. He wrote home to his mother to let her know he would be delayed. In the next week we fell into step with one another as if we had been made for each other. It was as if two halves of a whole came together.

My family did not approve. They were cold and silent when we told them we were getting married. They said nothing as I packed a suitcase. They remained silent as I walked down the lane. I knew they would not want me back.

We could have been married by a military chaplain the next day. But I wanted to be married before nightfall.

The Baptist minister refused. He said my daddy would have to come ask.

The Methodist minister agreed. Knowing he had a daughter a little younger than me, it might have helped that I asked one question.

"Reverend, if you had a daughter who was leaving home to be with the man she loved, wouldn't you want her to be married before dark?"

We sent a telegram to my husband's mother to let her know the good news, and that we were on the way. We stopped at a photography studio to have our photograph taken. Two days later, we stepped off the bus in his home town.

I was nervous. I'd never been away from home. My husband had assured me his mother would love me like the daughter I now was. It was his idea that I stay with her until he returned from the war.

My mother-in-law was quiet and met me with brittle reserve. I told myself she was shy and that we needed time to come to know each other. She was, after all, full of smiles and fond touch for my husband.

A week later my husband boarded the bus to return to his unit. The day he left he brought home presents. Mine was a royal blue cardigan sweater. His mother had one of deep gold.

"To keep my girls warm while I'm away," my husband smiled.

He was happy to see how pleased we were with our gifts.

The three of us walked arm-in-arm to the bus station. I hated to see him go. No doubt his mother felt the same. I tried to smile as much as I could, wanting him to remember me wearing a smile and the gift he bought for me.

We waved our good-byes even as the bus

turned the corner. It was not yet out of sight when my mother-in-law spun on me in a fury.

"Do you think I don't see what you're doing?"

I was stunned at her rage.

"You bitch! Do you think I am going to stand by and let my son waste his life on some backward timber trollop? I've already hired a lawyer to have this ridiculous marriage annulled. For all I know you're not really married, anyway."

She leaned in menacingly and lowered her voice.

"And if you're knocked, I don't want to know about it."

She turned and stormed off in the direction of home.

I was speechless. The dust thrown by the bus had yet to settle. I could hear its engine shifting gears just down the road. And my whole world had just collapsed.

I must have been a sight. No doubt my eyes were wide and my mouth hanging open. I just stood there in my new, blue sweater.

I returned to the house, and tried to never leave my room when my mother-in-law was there. I tried to be invisible.

She hated that I was her son's room.

I wrote to my husband to tell him that things were not working out as planned. I told him I would find a job and write when I had found a new place to live.

But I couldn't find a job. No one would hire me. Everywhere I went I could see people huddle together, whisper, point, and cast sidelong glances in my direction.

My mother-in-law was skilled in her efforts to drive me away. There was no telling what rumors she had spread.

I was in my room one morning when heard someone knock at the front door. My mother-in-law spoke briefly to a man. The door closed and I heard the sound of someone walking back toward the street.

A shriek from the living room shot me off my bed and down the stairs. My mother-in-law was distraught. She was rocking back and forth on the couch, her eyes wild. At her feet were a crumpled envelope and a yellow telegram.

I picked up the telegram. It had been addressed to me. My heart sank and I read the single line telling me the love of my life had been killed in the line of duty.

I remember lying on my bed, clutching the

telegram to my heart. I don't remember crying, but I must have. I don't remember eating. I don't remember how long I lay there. I remember dark, followed by light, but not how many times. It was all a blur.

My mother-in-law came into my room without knocking. She was wearing a new Sunday dress. She told me to get up and meet her at the funeral home in two hours. She said we had a funeral to plan.

Her voice was quiet and cold as she said, "You should pick out the casket."

She was right, of course. Briefly, I thought it must be odd to go to a funeral home on a Sunday, but it also seemed to be appropriate. I was really not up to questioning anything.

I washed my face and tried to tidy my hair. In the mirror I saw a wild, crushed thing looking back at me. Thinking that no one would be expected to look her best while making funeral arrangements, I slipped on a clean dress, leaving my best dress in the closet. For comfort more than warmth, I took my blue sweater from the back of the door, and set off down the street.

When I arrived at the funeral home I thought I must have come at the wrong time. A funeral was just ending. People were exiting the front door, stopping to offer condolences to the woman standing there.

It was my mother-in-law.

I came to a stop on the sidewalk in front of the funeral home. People began to notice me. Some refused to look at me. Others gave me all manner of dirty looks. They walked a wide circle around me as they headed toward a tented site near an open grave in the adjoining cemetery.

Following a friend's pointed gaze, my mother-in-law turned to look at me. In her arms she held the precisely-folded flag meant for a widow of a fallen soldier. It could go to the mother if there was no spouse. She also held three cases I knew would contain posthumously-awarded medals.

To this day I have never seen such a look of cold triumph as was on my mother-in-law's face. She, alone, had planned and conducted my husband's funeral. I never learned what she said to others, or how she managed to make arrangements without me.

She reveled in her cruel victory for a moment before moving toward the car waiting for family to follow the hearse to the grave site. I turned to see a casket, between pallbearers I did not know, slide into the open door of the hearse.

Tears filled my eyes as I looked at the casket. A knife of perception cut through my heart. My husband was in there. He was so near, and yet so far.

Feeling faint, I stumbled to the nearest tree at the edge of the property. I tried to stand behind the trunk out of sight, reaching toward it for support. I crumpled to the ground, in spite of my best efforts.

A woman soon stood beside me. I looked up to see the minister's wife. I remembered her from the one time we all had been to church together. Alarm and concern showed on her face. In her eyes were questions and confusion.

"She asked me to meet her here to plan the funeral," I tried to explain. "She said I should pick out the casket."

It was then, as I pulled the sweater close around me, that I saw the holes. My beautiful sweater had been repeatedly sliced by the sharp edge of a knife or scissors. My heart felt as if it had been stabbed as many times as my sweater. I heard a wrenching sob escape my throat.

The situation became clear to the minister's wife. She looked over her shoulder to watch my mother-in-law as she slid into the back seat of the waiting car.

Turning back to me, her lips in a grim line of contempt, the minister's wife spoke softly.

"I wonder if you might do something for me."

I looked up at her as she bent down next to me. The kindness in her eyes shocked me. It had been so long since I had seen anything but harshness when anyone looked at me.

"In a week my husband and I will be moving to a new church. He's gone there now to make arrangements. I wonder if you would come stay with me for a few days. I'm not used to being alone."

All I could do was look into those gentle eyes and nod. I never wanted to see my mother-in-law again. She surely didn't want to see me. A place to go, even for a few days, would be most welcome.

"Let me go with you to collect your things," the woman in front of me said. "You may as well bring all you own."

She helped me up and linked her arm in mine as we walked to my husband's room. While everyone was at the grave site, she helped me to pack my things. We were out of the house before the services ended.

I've never gone back.

The next thing I remember is sitting at the kitchen table in the little parsonage. The minister's wife tried to talk with me, but I wasn't much of a conversationalist.

I'm rather ashamed of myself at that. She was so nice to me.

Somehow a bowl of hot vegetable soup found its way in front of me. The smell was thoroughly tempting. I did not know how many days it had been since I had last eaten.

My mind began to clear a bit, and I felt stronger. I ate most of the soup and a piece of bread with butter. I drank a glass of water, and a cup of hot tea.

"I'm running a hot bath for you," said the minister's wife as she refilled my teacup. "Use all the soap and shampoo you like. Soak until you are a prune. When you're finished we can have some girl talk over hot chocolate in our pajamas."

We never made it to girl talk. After a long, hot bath I combed my freshly-washed hair and slipped into my nightgown. The minister's wife was waiting for me on the couch with a cup of hot chocolate for each of us on the coffee table.

I sat down on the comfortable couch, looked at the hot chocolate placed so thoughtfully in front of me. How different it was for me to be treated with courtesy and kindness. Just as I opened my mouth to say so, the surface that had held me up cracked open and dropped me into a well of anguish and loss. I did not know a body could feel so much pain.

I began to cry in a way I never had. I couldn't help it. I wailed from the depths of my soul. It was as if something terrible inside me needed to break loose and come out.

Grief can be an avalanche at the most awkward times.

The minister's wife slid across the couch and put her arm around my shoulders. It was a comfort.

"I've been waiting for this," she said. "It's about time. Cry all you want to."

I did. I cried then, and after I went to bed. When I woke during the night, I cried again.

At the first light of dawn I woke to a fresh day. Grief remained. But the tears had mostly gone. And I knew I had to figure out where to go from there. Hearts don't heal in a town full of hard glances and harsh whispers. The one person who had behaved well toward me would soon be moving away. Leaving was my only option.

I washed, dressed, and headed down the stairs. The boards creaked slightly as I quietly descended.

The minister's wife appeared at the kitchen door wearing a blue and white day dress and a welcoming smile. I hadn't seen such a smile since my husband stepped onto the bus.

"Do you like coffee in the morning, or tea?" she asked. "I have both."

"I'll have whatever you are having," I replied as I followed her into the kitchen. There I saw a table already laid for breakfast and a meal in the works.

The minister's wife poured a cup of tea and set it near one of the plates. Glasses of orange juice and water were already at each table setting.

"I don't know if the next parsonage will have a waffle iron," she said, her eyes gleamed impishly as she continued. "So I'm making good use of this one before I give it up."

"How can I help?" I asked.

The minister's wife gestured toward the table.

"Everything is almost done. You sit down. Later you can help me, if you like. I could use some company while packing."

"I can help with that," I assured her.

Honestly, I wanted to be busy.

The next moment I found myself staring at a large waffle topped with strawberries and maple syrup. The fragrance was captivating.

"Eat!" the minister's wife encouraged, as she

sat down in front of her own full plate, gesturing with flare. "This is a breakfast to enjoy!"

Flavors burst onto my tongue at first bite. I thoughtfully explored each one. My mother-in-law had begrudged me every morsel of food and drink I consumed. I resorted to drinking a lot of water. Glancing at the hand that reached across my plate to the orange juice, I noticed how thin I had become. Without realizing, I had begun to keep my ring finger curled so as to not lose my wedding ring.

Embarrassed at being quiet for so long at the table, I apologized.

"I'm sorry. I guess I'm not a good conversationalist just now."

"Oh, don't you worry about a thing," replied the minister's wife with a flip of her hand and a smile. "Any time someone appreciates my food the way you do, I'm content."

"I do thank you for it," I assured her. "It's the best I've had in a very long while."

"Thank you," she said, placing a hand on her chest and making a slight seated bow. "I'm honored."

We ate in silence before the minister's wife quietly asked what we both had been thinking.

"What will you do now?"

I looked into her concerned eyes for a moment before honestly replying.

"I don't know."

"Do you have people of your own?" she asked.

"Not really," I replied. "I was fairly well disowned for marrying a man thought to be just passing through. And even if I wanted to go back, it's so far away."

Staying in town was not an acceptable option. That was clear.

With more resolve than I felt, I squared my shoulders.

"I will leave. I will find a new place and make it my own."

"You are a woman of courage," the minister's wife said quietly. "Most of us would fall apart in your shoes."

"My husband and I never talked about what to do if this happened," I continued. "I think he believed I would be welcome in his home. And I never heard from him after I wrote to tell him living there wasn't working out. In fact, I never heard from him at all. I wrote every day, but he never wrote back."

"I think he did," said the minister's wife as

she rose from the table.

Stepping out onto the back porch, she retrieved a small bundle that fit into the palm of her hand. The scent of stale fire entered the room as she placed a handkerchief streaked with soot in front of me. She took away my plate to make room.

I unwrapped the cloth to find fragments of burned letters. Some of the envelopes displayed my name on the address. Others could no longer be read, but the unburned, folded fragments contained words of love, plans for the future, and encouragement. But the letters were so burned that not a single sentence was left complete. Only one or two words on each line could be read in the small spaces between the crumbling, blackened edges of the paper.

"I found those in the fire while you were packing," explained the minister's wife. "I didn't know if I should tell you. But I think you should know that your husband did think of you, and he did write."

I thought of the way my mother-in-law had made a point to sit in front of a fire most evenings, even when the night was warm. I had not understood her need for the fire. Nor had I understood the peculiar way she had looked at me. It was a mix of hate, revenge, and sadness. Sometimes she looked at me with a cruel smile under sad eyes when I walked into the room.

Now I understood. She had been reading, and then burning my letters.

"How could anyone be so mean?" I whispered, feeling a fresh slash in my wounded heart. "This is purely hateful."

"I no longer even try to understand the ways of cruelty," said the minister's wife. "But I do try to recognize it when I see it. And I try to do what I can about it."

"Is everyone as nice as you where you come from?" I asked with a smile.

"Missouri?" the minister's wife smiled in return. "We tend to be nice folks. People there tend to be polite and neighborly."

"It sounds like a good place. Maybe I'll go there," I pondered.

"You are right to leave here," she continued. "For you, this town is a poisoned well."

"I'll leave tomorrow," I said as I wrapped the handkerchief back around the burned letter fragments.

"Can you stay another day or two?" asked the minister's wife. "My husband and I talked on the telephone last night. He wants to stop to visit a chaplain he knows. Together, they are trying to see what they can do for you. He will be home in a few days."

With tears in my eyes, I nodded my consent to staying as I stood, carefully holding my husband's words in my hand. I had nowhere to go. Staying another couple of days would make no matter.

"Do you want to keep those?" asked the minister's wife, nodding toward the precious bundle in my hand.

"Yes," I said, holding the pouch of charred fragments in both hands.

"Let me find an envelope for you," she offered. That might help you to keep them safe."

She left me alone in the room as she went into her husband's office. I heard a drawer open and close. She was soon back next to me with a clean envelope and a memorial card from my husband's funeral service.

"Here you go," she said kindly, handing the envelope to me, and then the card. "Slip this inside. It will keep the envelope sturdy, and help preserve your letters."

Once the letter fragments were securely in the envelope, I shook the bits of charred paper that had crumbled into the handkerchief into the trash. The handkerchief was badly stained.

"May I keep this, too?" I asked.

I knew the handkerchief was ruined. And I

felt it should remain with my letters, although I still don't know why.

"Of course," the minister's wife wore a smile again.

Over the next two days we packed personal belongings, and then cleaned the parsonage in preparation for the next family to occupy. I enjoyed the light conversation that came with the cleaning and packing. I also had plenty of time to think.

In the evenings the minister's wife and I played board games and drank tea. My heart began to lighten for moments at a time, and once I even noticed myself in the middle of a small laugh. From the look on the minister's wife's face, I could see she had been pleased to finally have engineered it.

On the third evening, as I spread out a board game for us to play, the minister's wife pressed money into my hand.

"Take this," she said. "You have earned it."

"I cannot take money from you," I protested.

"The Church allows for a cleaning woman to come in to prepare for the transition between families at the parsonage. You cleaned. You are entitled to the money allotted for that task. You have earned it."

I folded the money in my hand and thanked

her for it. In my ponderings as to my next steps, I knew I had no money to spend. I didn't have even one dime. Now I would be able to make a few choices. The bills felt good in my skirt pocket, next to the buttons I had removed from my ruined sweater.

Two days later the minister arrived home. He smiled warmly and took my hand in his own large one.

"I'm sorry for your loss," he said.

Sadness and concern rested in his eyes, and I knew he meant it.

As he hung his coat, he withdrew a narrow paper from the breast pocket. Turning toward me he extended an envelope.

"A military chaplain friend of mine was able to expedite matters. I explained your circumstances. He asked that I relay his condolences, and this."

I lifted the flap on the envelope. Two checks were inside.

"One of those is your husband's pay. The other is your widow's benefits," the minister explained. "It is good that he took the time to register you as his beneficiary so quickly. Otherwise, these benefits might have gone to another."

We both knew who he meant. His mother might still be expecting what I held in my hand.

I withdrew the checks from the envelope. I saw my name on the payee line, just after I glanced at the date. My eyes returned to the date.

"When were these checks written?" I asked.

"Just yesterday," explained the minister, pointing to the date line on the check.

Yesterday had been my eighteenth birthday. It had not crossed my mind.

"In the morning I'll take you to the bank so you can open an account," offered the minister.

"No," I said thoughtfully. "I'd like to cash these."

"That's a lot of money," the minister said in a tone of doubt and caution. "You'll want to keep it safe."

"Yes," I agreed. "But I am leaving. And I don't want to return."

The minister nodded his understanding.

"We will go first thing in the morning."

That night I didn't sleep very well. I was up before dawn, and decided to pack my suitcase. Then I went downstairs to make coffee.

As I searched the kitchen for breakfast possibilities, the minister's wife stepped into the kitchen.

"Do you know how nice it is to wake up to the smell of brewing coffee?" she asked.

If I'd had any fears about snooping around another woman's kitchen, that was the end of them. Her smile was warm and genuine, even if still a little bit sleepy.

"I wasn't sure what to use for breakfast," I said as I closed a cupboard. "Rationing being what it is, I didn't know how you had meals planned."

"No one will be in this house for at least a week. We should use anything that could spoil," she replied.

"Eggs and toast?" I asked.

The minister's wife nodded. Coming into the kitchen, she took an apron from the back of the door, and reached into the cupboard for the eggs and bread.

"I could find some greens to chop into the eggs," I offered. "It would make them go farther, and give them some flavor."

"That would be nice," she smiled. "I'd like to hold back an egg."

Walking down the back porch steps I

remembered I was not in familiar territory. Plants were a little bit different here. I didn't even recognize some of them, and hadn't seen some of my trusted staples. It was a relief to find a few handfuls of dandelion, violet, and young plantain leaves. Those would do nicely.

Breakfast was pleasant. The minister commented on the greens, saying they were an inspirational turn in times of shortages of food and spices.

I don't know if that meant he liked the taste, or not.

The dishes done and my suitcase next to the front door, the minister and I walked to the bank. I was glad for such respectable company in the town that had pointedly shoved me out and left me alone. No one would behave badly in front of the minister. But I'm sure we both noticed how people we passed wished him a good morning, and said nothing to me.

Once we entered the bank the minister called a morning greeting to the single teller behind the counter, who was immediately oriented toward customer service. He asked how he could help on such a fine morning.

The minister, smiling expectantly, nodded to me.

"We have checks to cash."

The teller's face fell as he looked at me. He didn't say a word.

The minister motioned for me to hand my checks to the teller, and I did. I was a little bit embarrassed when he handed them back for me to endorse. I didn't quite know how to go about it. I'd never cashed a check before. But I managed, with the minister's guidance.

Our next stop was the bus station, which was also the town gas station and service garage. The owner came to the counter, cleaned his hands with a rag, and smiled at me.

"I thought I might see you sometime soon, young lady. Where would you like to go?"

"Missouri," I replied.

"What city?" he asked.

I had no idea.

The man behind the counter paused with me for a moment, before taking a ticket from the drawer in front of him. He began to write.

"This one will take you to St. Louis, Columbia, and Kansas City. Maybe you'll find what you want along the way to one or the other. You can find connections to just about anywhere in the state from any of those cities."

"That will be fine," I said, smiling at him as I

paid for the ticket.

"Your bus leaves in an hour," he said.

Tucking the ticket into my purse among so many paper dollars and coins, I never felt so rich. I was tempted to clutch the handbag against my chest to keep it safe. But that seemed silly. So I slid the strap over my arm, and said a cheerful goodbye to the man behind the counter.

His pleasant treatment of me felt like a gift. I'd seen him around town, but couldn't recall an actual conversation with him. He probably heard everything about everybody as customers came and went from his establishment.

"Missouri?" the minister asked as we walked up the porch steps of the parsonage.

"I've come to believe some very nice people must be there," I said. "Missouri seems like a better place to start than others might be."

I couldn't argue with you," the minister chuckled as he opened the door.

Across my suitcase lay a loose-fitting coat, gloves, and a hat. They were perfect for travel. My small wardrobe held nothing of the kind.

Hearing us enter, the minister's wife appeared in the foyer.

"I hope you don't mind second-hand," she

said. "I doubted you would have time to shop. And I don't want to take all I own to the next place. If you would take these things, I would be grateful."

She had a way of making her own generosity come across as though a person was doing her a favor. How could anyone refuse?

"I'm the one who's grateful," I told her. "Thank you."

The minister suddenly reached into the pocket of his coat.

"I almost forgot!" he exclaimed as he handed a slip of paper to me. "This is the name and address of the chaplain I mentioned. When you are settled somewhere, contact him. He will help you arrange for the monthly checks to be sent to you there. His telephone number is there, too, in case you are near a telephone."

"Thank you," I murmured as I slipped the paper into my purse.

"And here is the address where we will be," the minister's wife said as she extended a card. "We would like to hear from you as often as possible. Please write to us there."

I promised I would.

"I'm going to say good bye to you now, my dear," the minister said as he moved toward the door. "There are some members of the congregation to see before we leave."

I shook his hand and thanked him for all he had done for me.

He tipped his hat with a smile, and left.

Turning to the minister's wife, I could see tears in her smile. Parting would not be easy.

"Maybe I should go," I said. "I'd like to stop at the general store for something to eat on the bus, and maybe something to read. And if I'm early I'll have my pick of the seats."

"Oh, I almost forgot! I have these for you," she exclaimed, disappearing in the kitchen for a moment. "It's only a little to keep you going. There just isn't much left."

Opening the napkin she handed to me, I saw one hard boiled egg, two carrot sticks, and four biscuits. I knew it was all she had.

"I can't take all your food!" I protested.

"Oh, yes you can!" she replied. "We will be leaving this afternoon. And if there is no food in the house, it's a good reason for my dear husband to take me out for lunch."

Donning my new coat, I slipped the food into one pocket and gloves into the other. Walking to the mirror on the wall, I checked my look in the hat. I liked it.

"You're beautiful," the minister's wife said. "I don't know if you know that."

I didn't. My husband had commented that I was a pretty girl, but no one had ever said I was beautiful. I wondered if it was the hat.

Before I left, I hugged the minister's wife and thanked her as well as anyone could. I promised to write, and I meant it. Suitcase in hand, I waved good bye from the front steps and set off for the general store.

Knowing I would never return, I tried to take in all I could of my last view of the town. I avoided looking at people. But I did see the sign posted on the general store window advertising a room to rent, complete with board, in a "comfortable home" owned by a "respectable widow." My mother-in-law's address was on the bottom of the sign.

I wished her a renter just like her.

The daughter of the store owners was behind the counter as I entered. We exchanged shy smiles. No one else was in the store. I breathed a sigh of relief.

Finding nothing to read, I selected a notebook, loose writing paper, envelopes, two pencils, and a small pocket knife for sharpening. I could begin a diary, and those letters I promised to send to my good friends. I thought about sending one to my parents. It wouldn't matter if I had no return address. They wouldn't write back.

When I placed my little pile of purchases on the counter, the young woman at the register slid the knife away from the rest.

"You won't need this," she said.

Reaching under the counter, she brought out a pocket knife. Silently, she set it down in front of me.

It looked familiar. I picked it up to feel it in my hand. As I examined the pocket knife I realized I did know it. My husband had carried this knife.

Gasping in surprise, I looked at the woman behind the counter.

She held forward another small object for me to take. As I reached toward her outstretched hand, she dropped something cool and solid into my open palm. It was a wedding ring I knew not long, but well.

I may have uttered a little cry as I looked to her for an explanation.

"She brought these here to trade," she said. "But you should have them. What happened to you isn't right."

It occurred to me that I had never before been alone in the store with this woman. How I wished we had been able to talk before the day I left.

"What will you say?" I asked, still looking at the articles in my hand. "Will you be in trouble?

"For giving you what is rightfully yours?" she asked. "No. Besides, I'm leaving soon, myself. By this time next week, I'll be living with a cousin and going to business school."

Had there not been a counter between us, I'm sure I would have hugged her. I thanked her profusely, and sincerely wished her well as I paid for my purchases. The ring, knife, and change went into my pocketbook at the same time.

My husband's personal effects had been returned, but intercepted. I wondered what else had escaped me.

I wondered if my mother-in-law had read my letters, or if she immediately burned them. One may have held the narrow braid of hair my husband had requested. The smell of burning hair would serve her right.

I could see the bus down the street as soon as I left the store. It had arrived at the station. My gaze did not waver I walked toward it. Once my suitcase had been stored in the luggage hold, I boarded to find I had my choice of seats. I selected one for the best view, but never looked out the window until we were well out of town.

I'd had enough of that place.

I still remember the comfortable cadence of the engine, the sturdy movement of the bus as the driver shifted up and down through the gears at each little town, and the steady sounds on the roads between. We stopped at most of those little towns to take on new passengers, or to let off one or two.

In the early afternoon the bus drove to a gas station. The driver announced we would have a fifteen minute break. It was a good time to eat a little bit of food from my napkin, find a privy, and purchase a small cup and a capped bottle at the general store next door. I had just filled the bottle with water from the outdoor spigot at the gas station when the bus driver called for the passengers to reboard.

The last passenger on the bus was a woman about my mother's age. Clutching her purse in both hands, she uneasily scanned the rows of seats as she slowly moved down the aisle. With so many rows empty, I was a little bit surprised when she stopped at the seat next to mine.

"Please excuse me," she said. "But would you mind if I sit next to you? Among so many men on this bus, I would appreciate feminine company."

With a quick glance, I realized we were the only two women there. I removed my hat from the seat next to me and smiled.

"Please do," I said. "I would like that, too."

With a sigh of gratitude, the woman sat down. The manner in which she straightened her dress and arranged her hat and purse on her lap seemed practiced, as did the way she settled into her seat.

"Do you travel often?" I asked, looking for a way to begin polite conversation.

"I'm afraid I do," the woman responded. "After my husband died I moved in with my sister. I try to be useful. But her husband doesn't want me there. So I have been taking the bus to visit relatives."

"Oh," I said. "I'm sorry."

The woman next to me patted my hand.

"Don't be," she said. "That's over. I'm on my way to accept a position as a lady's companion. We've been corresponding. We're both widows, and neither of us wants to be alone. She lives in comfortable circumstances. There will be plenty of room, and enough to do. We may even go abroad, or at least see the country."

How bright and easy my new acquaintance had become. She had something to look forward to. I was happy for her. As I murmured my response I also recognized I was envious. Until that moment I hadn't understood how much I could use something in life to regard with hopeful anticipation.

Seeing my purse below my hand, the woman next to me leaned toward me to whisper.

"My dear, you never know what may happen with a purse. If you have money I would advise you to keep it safe in your shoe," she suggested before she leaned a little closer. "That's what I do."

I thanked her for her advice. It was a good idea.

The woman beside me filled our row with pleasant and excited chatter as she spoke of the plans she and her new employer had discussed. At times she shrugged her shoulders and actually giggled with glee at one or another of the circumstances or events she would soon experience.

I was glad for her. An air of despair still clung to her. Lines of sadness had worn themselves into her gentle face. She must have been unhappy for a long time. I found hope for myself in her turn toward better.

At sunset the bus pulled into another gas station, and the driver announced a thirty-minute break for supper. Next door the staff of a small café, under a hotel of no more than four rooms, had clearly been waiting for our arrival. They all stood waiting at the door.

The last two off the bus, I turned to the

woman next to me. She wasn't looking to the door of the café, but well past it. A fine automobile waited there. A man in a chauffeur's livery exited the driver's door and walked toward us.

"Oh, there's the man sent for me. I'm so glad he's here in time," the woman beside me whispered in excitement. "Isn't it all so very elegant?"

I had to admit it was. But I don't think she heard much from me from then on. She joined the chauffeur, who spoke to the bus driver about which cases to remove from the cargo hold of the bus. I expressed my best wishes. She returned a smiling, flustered farewell. And then she was gone. As I took a seat in the little café, I looked through the window in time to see the chauffeur assist the eager woman into the back seat of the car. As the car drove away, I sent silent wishes for continued happiness along with her.

A woman near my own age came to take my order. From the speed at which she moved, and the choices she offered, it was clear the café was prepared to serve patrons well in time to finish a meal before the bus departed. I ordered a thick soup and a simple sandwich. She returned almost right away with the soup and a glass of water. I poured most of the water into my water bottle. The soup was almost gone when my sandwich arrived. I cut it into fourths and ate one section. The rest went into the napkin the minister's wife had given to me, and into my coat pocket with the rest of the food I had saved.

There was no way to know what lay ahead.

I had not eaten out very often, and never alone. As I prepared to leave I became aware I knew little about tipping waitresses. It had something to do with ten percent of the price of the meal and quality of service. I wasn't sure what to do. But I had to go. Leaving a quarter under the edge of the plate, I hoped it would be adequate. My bill was just under a dollar.

At the counter next to the cash register was a rack of items travelers might need. An idea sparked as I spotted a pack of two needles and a little spool of white thread. I bought them.

Turning from the counter I glanced back at the table I left in time to see the young woman who had brought my food take away the empty plate. She paused in amazement as she slowly picked up the quarter. Delight spread across her face. I smiled at her before I left, and spent no more time worrying about the gratuity.

The little café had a ladies' room. And since I was the first one of the passengers to pay for my meal, I knew I had a little time. Removing some of the larger currency from my purse, I folded them to fit snugly into my shoes. I thought it would be more uncomfortable than it was. But I cautioned myself to not kick off my shoes during the night.

Fishing though my pockets, I found the soot-stained handkerchief that had belonged to the minister's wife. I folded it in half. Quickly unbuttoning my skirt, I let it fall almost to the floor. With needle and thread in one hand, and the handkerchief in the other, I basted a small pocket to my slip just below the waistline. I slipped in the rest of the largest denominations. Even more of my money would be safe.

With the money safely against my belly, I pulled my skirt back into place. After closing the button at the waistband, I was dismayed to notice the money in the new pocket of my slip showed as a small bulge. Smoothing my skirt made no difference. It would soon be time to board the bus again, and I had no chance to move the pocket.

Then I realized the bulge was more of a blessing than a difficulty. I still wore a wedding band. A lot of women my age had small bulges just below their waistbands. Assumptions would land far from a freshly-basted pouch holding money. Smiling, I patted my belly, donned my coat and hat, and slid my purse strap over my arm. Feeling a little more prepared for whatever lay ahead, I was ready to go.

In the dark of the night, low light glinted from the edges of the metal bus. The wide whitewalls of the tires fairly glowed. Near the open door the bus driver stood next to a man in the same uniform. As I approached they shook hands, bid each other a good night, and parted. The new driver tipped his hat as I approached the door, and boarded after me. Soon we were off again.

With only darkness outside my window, I decided I should try to sleep. It was the first time I had tried to sleep sitting upright without my husband's shoulder as a pillow. For that reason, and ever so many more, I wished he were still with me. I thought of taking off my coat and rolling it into a pillow, but the night was becoming cold, and I didn't want to smash my food in the pockets. We stopped only twice during the night. No one seemed to sleep well. I nibbled another section of my sandwich.

As the light of dawn began to fill the bus, we stopped at another little town with a gas station next to a café under a hotel. This one was larger than the last. A sign advertising a breakfast special of pancakes and eggs caught my eye. It sounded perfect, to me.

Traveling by bus was becoming familiar. So were the little stops along the way. But the comfort had gone out of it. I was wearing the same clothes I had been wearing a morning ago. Sitting for so long was not something I was used to. And I still had no idea where I was going to stay.

After breakfast, more people than usual boarded the bus. An older man, dressed better than most in a dark wool topcoat, removed his hat when he reached the seat next to mine.

"Would you mind if I sit next to you, Miss?" he asked.

"Please do," I said. "It would be nice to talk with someone."

"Our weather is taking a turn, it seems," he said as he settled into his seat.

"I'm new to the area," I responded with a smile. "I wouldn't know what to expect one way or another."

"How far will you be going?" the man asked gently.

"To Missouri," I replied.

"Why, Miss! You're in Missouri already!" the man told me. "You've been in Missouri for a while."

I hadn't known. Nothing more than the name of the town had been on all those little signs I had seen along the way.

"Oh!" I said in surprise, and turned to look out the window, now that I was where I had intended to go.

After a moment the man beside me spoke again.

"You'll like Missouri," he said. "We have the best of everything here, and the nicest people you will ever meet."

"That's good," I said turning back to him. "I'm looking for a place to make a home."

Too polite to voice the questions that showed on his face, the man next to me continued.

"Yesterday I drove in from the City. Last night I stayed at my sister's place. We're taking care of my aunt's house. She just passed away."

"Oh, I'm sorry!" I said.

"Don't be," the man next to me assured. "She was old, and had lived life mostly on her own terms. She finished her spring planting, went to church the next day, and then came to visit my sister. That's where she passed away. She had a good life, and often said so."

"I'm honestly happy for her," I said.

"Thank you," the man next to me smiled. "She lived in the town where my sister and I grew up. My father was the undertaker there. But that wasn't the life for me, so I studied law and moved to the City. I'm only coming back to make arrangements to sell her house."

I nodded that I understood, and searched for something to contribute to the conversation. I thought about asking what city the man had come from, assuming it was one of the three mentioned on my bus ticket. But I didn't want to seem as ignorant as I was.

"What is your little town like?" I asked.

"Oh, it's quiet, friendly, and steady," the man next to me explained. "It has a general store, a school, a couple of churches, and a bank. New businesses are coming in, and there is talk of opening a library."

As the man next to me pleasantly went on about the nearing town, he slipped from present to past, relating tales from his childhood. Clearly he enjoyed the chance to stroll through his memories with a willing listener.

Nearing the edge of town the man suddenly leaned slightly in front of me to point out the window. He smelled faintly of witch hazel and bay laurel.

"There's my aunt's house," he said.

I looked to the small Victorian with the low front porch across the front. Freshly painted under a solid roof, it seemed to ache with loneliness.

"May I see it?" I heard myself ask, quite to my own surprise.

"Why, yes, Miss. But surely you understand a woman alone..." he began, looking to my left hand. "Oh. I see. War brings us to different ways, doesn't it?"

"It does," I quietly agreed.

The bus stopped at a gas station near the center of town. The driver announced a thirty-minute break for lunch at the hotel and restaurant next door.

I wasn't used to making big decisions in less than thirty minutes. I wasn't used to making big decisions at all. I looked at everything I could in that town as my latest traveling companion and I briskly walked down the street. He answered my questions and was full of comments on features he thought might be of interest.

I think the house had me the moment I heard the hollow fall of my first footstep on the planks of the front porch. Unlocked, the carved front door easily opened to a small, but comfortable entry, with rooms on each side. I moved through the first floor, taking in all I could.

I think I felt more than I saw. The man who came with me spoke of leaving the furniture and dishes, as his sister had already removed the items of family interest. He apologized for the lack of most modern conveniences, pointing out the pump at a wide sink in the kitchen, and the one electrical outlet his aunt had installed to accommodate a radio.

I was used to oil lamps and wood stoves.

The furniture was better than I had seen in most homes the entire time I had been a child. Once the man assured me there was a bed and linens upstairs, I asked how much he would like for the house.

He named the precise amount I had in my shoes. Seeing my surprise he misunderstood, and went on to say the house came with five acres. His aunt, he said, had sold the rest of her land when she became old. The timber in back of the wide lawn, garden plots, a barn, and small outbuildings would also be mine.

I agreed to the price.

With a smile, the man extended his hand, which I accepted. I'd heard a handshake was part of sealing a deal in business.

But I had no idea what else to do. I felt myself in the blur of unfamiliar territory, which I had traversed with great speed.

"Let's hurry back to the bus," the man encouraged. Before it leaves, we should collect your luggage. After the paperwork is done, I'll come back to start fires in the stoves for you."

I didn't know what paperwork had to be done, but I couldn't have agreed more about my suitcase. We arrived just in time for the driver to retrieve my only belongings from the luggage hold of the bus. With both hands on the valise handle, I watched the bus drive way, leaving only a brief swirl of road dust behind.

"The title office is by the courthouse," the man next to me said, reaching to carry my suitcase. "But it would be closed for the noon hour. Would you allow me to treat you to lunch while we wait?"

"I would like that," I said, listening to my rumbling tummy. "You could tell me more about this town, and the house. I'm eager to hear about the house."

"My grandparents were among the first to this area," he began. "Their cabin is in the woods behind the house, although I haven't seen it in a while. I couldn't tell you if the roof is still intact. My mother was young when they built the house by the road. Her sister, my aunt, never left. She lived there her whole life."

"There were just the two sisters?" I asked.

"No. They had a younger brother. He died in the Spanish American War. He was the first to be buried in the little family cemetery behind the orchard. My grandparents were next, then my parents, and now my aunt. I hope it doesn't bother you to have the family there. I doubt there will be any more of us. We all have plans to be buried elsewhere."

We arrived at the café and were seated right away. The man asked if he could order for me, and

I agreed. He asked our waitress for two of the specials described on a small blackboard inside the door. They arrived in no time. Out of habit I found myself scanning the plate for items to fit into the napkin in my pocket for later.

The man across from me at the table easily talked of the town. He told me its history, and of the people and businesses there. Now and then he would indicate one or another visible through the window of the café.

I was interested most in the house. I eagerly listened to all the man across from me had to say. He spoke of the history of the land and his family there. The barn had once held the finest teams of horses and mules in the area. On either side of a small creek was an orchard, still doing well. There was a chicken coop, which I had noticed. Beside it were a strawberry patch and a series of vegetable, herb, and flower gardens, which could be watered by a well under a windmill that the man promised to check before he left that day.

While the man paid our bill, I went to the ladies' room. There I retrieved the money from my shoes and slid it into the palm of my glove.

I suppose all went well at the title office. I signed where I was told, and placed the cash from my glove onto the table. Hearing that my husband's name could be added later, I smiled and nodded, not saying a word.

In a way I knew I was being untruthful by not mentioning my widowhood. I didn't see that it hurt anyone. And, to be honest, it felt comforting to behave as if my husband would come home and join me in the little house beyond the edge of town.

"I'm happy the house has gone to fine people like you," the man said as we walked back to the house. "It's nice to know it will be in good hands from here on out."

A gust of chilled air blew under my loose coat. I clutched it tighter around me and looked up into darkening clouds filling the sky.

"It might be good to bring in more wood than usual. It looks like a storm is on the way," the man commented. "You might want to lay in a few supplies, too. I'm sure there is enough oil for the lamps, but I don't know about food."

"After so much time on a bus, I'll be happy for another walk this afternoon," I said.

In spite of his nice clothes, the man made sure the house and windmill water pumps were in working order, carried in firewood, showed me the particulars of operating the wood stoves to their best performance, and flipped back the rug in the pantry to show me the recessed ring to pull the door to the cellar below.

"My aunt extended the back porch over the well where the sink is now, and closed it in with windows to start plants in late winter. She covered the cellar door, and added a pantry above at the same time."

"She must have spent a lot of time in her kitchen," I speculated. "It's large, airy, and has plenty of space to work."

It was then that I spied what appeared to be a very small leather box on the kitchen table. Examining it, I looked questioningly at the man as he smoothed the pantry rug back into place.

"Oh," he laughed.

Taking the piece from my hand, he walked to the electrical outlet in the kitchen and slid it over the surrounding box.

"My aunt made this," he explained. "She said she didn't want the electricity to leak out."

"Your aunt must have been quite a woman," I smiled widely. "No doubt I'll be hearing more about her."

"No doubt you will. She definitely had her own way of going about life," the man agreed as he moved to a window to look at the sky. "I would like to stay and tell you more about her. But I don't relish the thought of walking back to meet the bus in a cold rain. I'll take my leave, and look forward to, perhaps, seeing you again."

"Of course," I said as we walked to the front

door. "Thank you for your kindness. I appreciate all you have done for me."

"My regards to your husband, Ma'am," the man said as he donned his hat.

Opening the front door reminded me of one thing we had forgotten.

"The keys!" I exclaimed. "You haven't given me the keys."

"The keys," the man repeated thoughtfully in the doorway. "I have no idea where they are. No one around here locks much of anything. There are keys to the house and some of the buildings. But where she kept them, I do not know."

"I'll look around," I assured him. "They might be in a drawer or hanging beside a doorframe."

The man gripped the brim of his hat to steady it against the wind. At the bottom of the porch steps he turned back to me.

"I'll ask my sister if she knows about the keys," he called against the wind as he looked upward. "Take care tonight, Ma'am. You're in for quite a bit of weather."

Closing the door against the wind, I felt the house begin to warm. I decided to take stock of what was on hand, and make a list of what I might need from the store. I might have time to make a quick trip to and back before rain began to fall.

In the kitchen cupboards were pans, dishes, glassware, and cutlery. Dried herbs hung from pins and strings across the ceiling of the enclosed porch. Soap rested in a dish by the sink. On the counter were canisters of flour and cornmeal. There was plenty of salt. The sugar and tea containers were empty.

The pantry held Ball and Mason jars filled with assorted vegetables and fruit. Additional jars held dried beans, peas, and corn. Sacks of flour and cornmeal were almost empty.

The cooler held nothing but bread gone moldy. The milk pitcher and butter dish were empty.

The top shelf of the cabinet below the stairs held lamp oil, candles in holders, and a tin containing boxed matches. On the second shelf was a jar of wicks, boxes of candles, a spare lamp shade, an outdoor lantern, and wall sconces.

Hoping to find fresh food before the storm landed, I quickly pulled on my hat and coat. Grabbing my purse from the table I spied a basket on the floor by the back door. Dumping out the twine and scissors inside, I gripped the handle and headed for the door.

The full cut of the coat did little to keep out the wind. I hurried as fast as I could in the cold gusts. By the time I rapidly pushed my way through the door of the general store I was fairly out of breath.

"I hope I'm not keeping you from safely going home before the thunderstorm arrives," I breathlessly said to the somewhat startled man behind the counter.

"No, Ma'am" he said with a finger pointed upward. "I live right upstairs. But you had best be quick about your shopping. I don't think it's a thunderstorm on the way. According to the signs, it's a spring blizzard about to land."

I had no experience with spring blizzards, but from the look on the man's face, it would be unwise to take them lightly. I quickly asked about bread, milk, eggs, butter, sugar, tea, and crackers. The storekeeper said he didn't have everything I wanted, but could give me what he had. He set about loading items into my basket on the counter, while I glanced around the store. Many of the items for sale were locally made. I paused to feel the soft wool of a receiving blanket and matching bonnet, but could waste no time at it. Money from my purse in hand, I faced the counter.

Barely waiting for my change, and with a quick warning toward care from behind the counter, I dashed back out into the cold wind, which had grown strong and damp. Before I reached my front porch, something not unlike tiny,

slushy snowballs hurled from the sky. They beat
my hat and soaked into my coat. Sharp wind
clawed at me as my wet gloves slid against the knob
to the front door. Once the door was open, a gust
pushed me inside. Leaning on the closed door
behind me, I was never so happy to be back
indoors.

I kicked off my wet shoes and carried them
to the kitchen. They would dry better there, along
with my hat and coat. Once they had been arranged
by the stove, I removed the contents of the basket
and set each item on the kitchen table. I would take
stock of what the shop owner had been able to
provide.

The wind above moaned and shrieked as I
lighted an oil lamp and placed a pan of water on the
stove. It occurred to me that I had never seen the
upstairs of my new home. There might be a
window open up there.

Grasping the oil lamp from the kitchen
table, I made my way to the narrow stairs. Wooden
treads, worn from years of use, made for an uneven
surface beneath my feet. As I moved higher in the
house I could hear ice against window glass and
roof, and gusts of wind that sometimes moaned
with a quality almost human.

From the small landing at the top of the
stairs I could see through the doorway of the rooms
on either side. I stepped into the room that must

have been the bedroom of the woman who had recently lived there. An iron bed stood under the slant roof, covered with a quilt and pillows. Beside it sat a straight chair and a bedside table holding an oil lamp on a small doily. On the other side of the room was a narrow wardrobe with dresser drawers down one side. Embroidered flour sack curtains covered a tightly-closed window.

The room across the hall must have been the spare room. Holding the lamp high in the doorway, I looked past the unmade bed to the window. It was closed. I stepped inside to see a room almost as simply furnished. A rocking chair sat on one side of the window. The night table was smaller than the one across the hall. The wardrobe was even narrower. Oddly, the blankets on the bed had been piled into the middle. The rest of the house had been so tidy. The dark heap on the bed in front of me seemed so out of place.

It moved. The pile of blankets moved. From within the dark heap a face turned to look at me.

With a cry of surprise, I nearly dropped the lamp. Alarmed, I took a step back. From the doorway I could see frightened eyes under tangled hair looking back at me. It was a young woman in the bed.

"Come up from there right now!" I ordered with more confidence than I felt.

Awkwardly, the young woman moved slowly away from me toward the edge of the bed. Her movements were heavy and labored. She grasped the iron footboard for support.

"Are you hurt?" I asked.

In the time it took for her to move the width of the footboard, I could see her difficulty. She was great with child. Her coat would not close in front of her. She must have been under the blankets to keep warm.

"You should come downstairs," I said. "The kitchen stove is lit. You would be more comfortable there."

The woman in front of me opened her mouth to respond, only to send out a scream as she doubled over in pain. She was in labor. I had thought her shrieks and moans to be part of the storm raging outside.

"How long has that been going on?" I asked.

"All day," she said as the pain subsided. "My water broke this morning. When I saw this place, I thought no one lived here."

"This morning no one did live here," I said as I moved beside her to help her down the stairs. "But now I do."

At the bottom of the stairs we removed her coat. She was too thin for the rumpled, dirty blue dress she wore over torn and scuffed shoes. Her dress nearly matched the dark circles faintly showing under her sunken eyes. I guessed she was a couple of years older than me.

"How long since you've eaten?" I asked.

"Yesterday," she said. "Maybe it was the day before."

I guessed whatever she had eaten wasn't much of a meal.

"Sit down," I said, gesturing toward the table. "I was about to eat a little something. We can share."

I'd been able to purchase milk in a pint jar at the store. I poured half of it into a glass, and filled it to the top with warm water. If this woman hadn't eaten much for a while, her stomach could reject food.

"Start with this," I said as I set the glass in front of her. "Go slow."

As I walked the rest of the milk to the cooler, I tried to remember all I knew about childbirth. It wasn't much. When it came to humans I only knew what I had overheard from older women as they talked. All of the births I had witnessed had taken place in a barn.

Nothing from the basket would make for a quick meal. I remembered the two quarters of my leftover sandwich in my coat pocket. The surrounding napkin was a little damp, which hid the beginning staleness of the bread. This was no time to be picky. Since the woman with me seemed to be keeping down the thin milk, I set a quarter of a sandwich on a plate in front of her, along with two of the four biscuits given to me by the minister's wife.

"See how you do with this," I cautioned her.

I sat at my own plate and watched her eat. She took small bites and chewed carefully. I guessed she knew more than a little bit about having too little food. When she thought I wasn't looking she tucked a biscuit into the pocket of her dress. I didn't say a word.

At her next contraction I scanned my memory of what to do.

"You should walk," I advised. "I've heard walking helps when the labor isn't too far along."

The woman at the table looked at me as if she didn't like that suggestion at all. But she reached for me to help her up, and began pacing back and forth across the kitchen.

Walking to the kitchen window by the sink, I looked into the storm outside. Dense snow furiously blew sideways. I couldn't see two feet past the glass.

"I don't know this town," I said to the woman behind me. "And I can't see a thing in this storm. How far away are your people?

She stopped and looked at me.

"My people?"

"Your husband. Your family," I began. "Wherever you were going."

"There is no husband," the young woman stated flatly as her eyes fell to the floor. "And my family doesn't want me...not like this. I have nowhere to go."

"Nowhere?" I asked incredulously. "Where have you been?"

"Once I began to show, my parents sent me to a home for wayward women. It was hell. Girls died. I ran away. I telephoned my mother, but she said I couldn't come home, not while I could still disgrace them."

She might have said more, but another contraction halted her explanation. She didn't really need to continue. Her story was one of many in that era.

I guessed that contraction had been harder than the rest. When it was over she looked at me with fear in her eyes. I suspect she saw the same in mine.

"How much do you know about having a baby?" I asked.

"Only what I've already done," she replied.

In no particular order I began to think of what we would need to do. I tried to think of all I had ever heard. Use button twist to tie the cord, and don't hurry to cut it. Some women squat in the corner, or deliver kneeling on their hands and knees. Press back a little bit on the baby's head to prevent tearing. Boil water. Wipe the baby's eyes, nose, and mouth. Tap its feet to make it cry. No need to hurry in bathing the baby. Make sure the afterbirth is intact.

What did that even mean?

I searched the house for anything to help with the task at hand. From towels, faded quilts, and an old saddle blanket from behind the kitchen door, I made a pallet that could be dragged to a corner if need be. I'd burn whatever couldn't be washed. But I did want to spare my dress and slip. All I owned fit into one suitcase. I intended to take those off when the time came, and suggested the soon-to-be-mother do the same.

After I set two of the softest towels for the baby near the stove, I poured a small amount of cooking oil from the pantry into a pan.

"What's that for?" I heard behind me.

"It's to massage your...where the baby comes out," I explained.

"Whatever for?" she asked.

"I've heard it softens and relaxes the opening," I said.

"That can't be true," she replied, grimacing into another contraction.

"If I were you, I wouldn't turn down anything that might be helpful," I advised.

When her contraction ended I gave her a glass of water to sip. That was the last thing I was sure I knew how to do. The next few hours scared us nearly to death. We hardly noticed the blizzard as it faded. But by the first light of dawn the sound of roaring, screaming wind no longer filled the house. Instead, we heard the newborn cry of a baby boy.

It seemed odd to me that the new mother didn't reach for her baby once I had cleaned, wrapped, and offered him to her. I thought she must be tired. She'd been through a lot.

"You should see if he's interested in feeding," I suggested. "Some babies need some encouragement."

She did no more than look at the baby I held forward. She didn't even smile.

"I've heard a baby at the breast helps the womb to take shape again," I said, trying a different tactic.

Looking me in the eye, she seemed to be trying to decide whether or not to believe me.

"How long will that take?" she asked, reluctantly taking the baby from me.

"I don't know," I shrugged. "A few days, at least."

She never seemed to warm up to the baby. I'd heard some women could feel low after their babies were born. She hadn't even named the baby. I thought she just needed some time.

I took care of the boy more than she did. It was me who lined an emptied dresser drawer with straw and soft cloths to place by the stove. It made a fine temporary crib, even if it didn't rock. And I gathered scrap cloth from around the house to make dresses and diapers. Sometimes I found myself lost in those beautiful eyes in that sweet, little face. But I tried to not become too attached. She would be leaving, and taking the baby with her.

I was washing her dress on the back porch when she appeared in the doorway, wearing one of mine. It was my second-best.

"The baby's been fed," she said. "He's asleep. I'm going for a walk."

It was a sunny day. All signs of the blizzard were gone, except for the mud made from the melted snow. Being out of the house to stretch her legs was a good idea. Maybe it would put a smile on her face.

It didn't. She returned a half-hour later looking no better. Maybe she was worse. She went upstairs without saying a word. I heard the springs on her bed squeak as she dropped down. She must have been tired.

That evening after supper we sat at the kitchen table over tea made from the last of the dried chamomile flowers that had hung from a string on the back porch. She had been silent through most of the meal.

"I telephoned my mother," she said when she finally spoke. "She said I could come home."

Immediately I clapped my hands and nearly jumped for joy. She had so wanted to be able to go home. I didn't know why she seemed so unhappy, until she continued.

"I can't bring the baby with me."

I hadn't been prepared for that. How could any mother want to separate another mother from her child? For a mother to even think to force such a separation between her own daughter and grandchild was beyond my comprehension.

"Oh," I said. "Well, you can stay here for a while. Once you have your bearings, you can start over somewhere else. If you wore a wedding ring, it might be easier for you."

Her expression was flat. She didn't like that idea.

"I suppose you could talk to one of the ministers in town," I tried again. "Maybe they know of a good couple who would raise your baby as their own."

I didn't really like that idea. Adopted children never seemed to hold the place in life as those born to a family. It was also true, in rare cases, that an adopted child was adored. It was an option, if she didn't want the baby. The idea of not wanting a baby was foreign to me, although I'd heard of it.

She nodded, said she would think about it, and went upstairs. I heard her moving around up there as I washed the dishes. By the time I went up, she was asleep in bed.

She was quiet the next day. I figured she was thinking about what to do. I was ironing her dress, shabby as it was, when she came to tell me she was going for a walk again. She still wore my second-best dress. I noticed she was beginning to fill it in a little bit better. She wasn't as thin as she used to be.

I thought she must have been gaining back some of her strength. She was gone longer than the day before and I took that to mean she had walked a little farther. She seemed stronger when she returned. Maybe it was resolve. Maybe she knew where she and the baby would be going. I didn't ask about something that was really none of my business.

I thought she might say something about a plan at supper. She didn't. She said very little. After tea made from the last of the spearmint leaves, she went upstairs to bed.

The next morning I woke to the sound of the baby crying. Opening my eyes to the first light of dawn on the horizon, I listened for my housemate to go to her child. She didn't. It wasn't the first time. Several times I was up in the night to check on the baby, change him, and take him to her to be fed. Sometimes I sat in the rocking chair to make sure she didn't fall asleep and smother him.

Across the hall I found an empty bed between me and the crying infant. I thought his mother must be out in the privy. I changed him, hushed him, and went downstairs with him to meet her as she came in. He was hungry.

Babe in arm, I stirred the coals in the kitchen stove, and dropped in another three pieces of wood. At the kitchen sink I filled a pan with water and set it on the stove.

When the boy's mother didn't return, I checked the privy, and the porches outside. I couldn't find her. Scanning the yard and street out front, I didn't see her anywhere.

Thinking she might have come downstairs in the night, and fallen asleep in one of the front rooms, went back inside. She wasn't there.

Rocking the fussy baby in my arms, I walked from one door way to the other, looking for his mother. I looked outside again, and then returned to go through the house.

It was then I noticed my hat and coat missing from the pegs where I kept them. Hers was there, but mine was gone. At first I thought she must have borrowed them, but then I noticed my shoes were missing, too. After walking through the wet and muddy yard, I had set my shoes by the door to dry. Now they were gone.

With a warning growing in the pit of my stomach, I lay the baby in his makeshift crib near the kitchen stove. I ran upstairs and pulled open the dresser drawers in her room. They were empty. But her dress was on the hook behind the bedroom door. At first the sight of the dress was a comfort, even if confused. Quickly, that comfort gave way to alarm.

Across the hall in my room I found that my dresses were missing. So were most of my underthings. Frantically, I looked for my personal papers at the back of the top, right dresser drawer. They were not there. They should have been right there on top of my wedding photograph. They were in the next drawer over. Someone had dropped them inside, but hadn't bothered to fold them neatly as I always did.

Unsettled and unsure, I scanned my bedroom. In my mind nothing had quite come together. But in an instant everything became clear. My suitcase was missing. It was then, with a lurch to my stomach, I knew for sure that she had gone.

The baby downstairs let out a cry, and my mind tried to wrap itself around the idea that his mother had left him behind. Leaving as she did, it seemed clear she didn't intend to return.

What was I going to do with an abandoned baby?

Back downstairs, I picked up the baby and walked to the front door again, knowing I wouldn't see his mother. She probably had left shortly after she last fed him. Nothing had come from looking up and down the street several times, but I did find one of my gloves at the edge of the porch. She must have dropped it as she hurried away. I picked it up and brought it back inside.

I dropped my glove on the kitchen table. There was my purse. It was open. I quickly picked it up to look inside. A couple of coins were still there. But all the paper money was gone. I was looking at the bottom of a nearly empty purse.

Placing a hand on my sick stomach, I was glad I had never taken the money from the pouch sewn to my slip, and that I had begun wearing it to bed after I had made shirts for the baby from my only nightgown.

Then I became angry. I fumed. How dare she? After all I had done for her!

The baby's wail interrupted my anger. He was hungry. I had to think of a way to feed him.

I scalded the half-pint of milk in the cooler. In desperation I also scalded my glove. I thought I might be able to feed the baby from one of the fingers, if I poked a needle hole in it. Later I would figure out what to do from there.

Hope against hope, it worked. It probably helped that he was that hungry. When he began to doze, I lay him in his dresser drawer cradle by the stove.

Before I rose I noticed a paper on the floor behind the table. I supposed it must have slid from the table top. I picked it up and began to read.

The lie. I read it over and over. The lie.

I was grateful to be so near a chair. In my hand I held a birth certificate. Dated the day before at the county courthouse, I read my husband's first name, my maiden name, and then my married name. That was the name of the baby. My maiden name had been written on the line for the mother's name, beside a forged signature. My husband's name, with a notation for his absence at war on the signature line, was given as the father's name.

I sat there for a long time. I realized I had never told the woman who had been there that I had been widowed. She had not asked a single question about me. She must have taken the information from my marriage certificate to complete the birth certificate. She must have also seen that I had papers from the Army, but not stopped to read them. With the war going on, she had made assumptions, as a lot of people would.

What was I to do with this little boy? Who would want an abandoned baby? These were hard times, and families often struggled to feed and clothe the children they already had.

Orphanages were places mentioned in horror stories. Formal adoption often led to the same. I had no faith in those possibilities. And I knew no one in town to trust.

I picked up the baby to hold him as I thought. His eyes opened. Confident and trusting, his gaze squarely met mine. It was then I knew. My heart opened up and took him in. He would be my son. I would take care of him.

I can't quite describe what came over me. It

might have been something like a mother's call to action. After removing one of the bills from the pouch basted against my slip, I pulled a dress that wasn't mine over my head, and slid my feet over pasteboard from a cracker box in shoes too big to otherwise fit. I felt like a rag-a-muffin. I wrapped my son against the light morning wind, buttoned myself into a shabby coat I had never worn, and set out to find what we needed. If I found nothing else, I had to find a way to feed my child.

My first stop was the general store. Gratefully, I found two women behind the counter. I explained I needed milk for my baby.

"Oh, dear! That can happen, particularly if you have had a shock," the older of the two said sympathetically as she directed the younger one to a cooler. "Have you had a shock?"

I replied that I had. I did not have to lie, which was good. I had not lived a life of lies, and wasn't comfortable with them.

In my haste, I had forgotten the basket. I wasn't even sure how to carry both a baby and a basket. I had a lot to figure out.

The store shelves held two glass baby bottles and three nipples. I said I would take them all. I could carry those in a small sack. We discovered two half-pint jars of milk would just fit, one each, into the pockets of my coat. There was no more to be had in the store. It wouldn't be enough.

The older woman asked me if I could wait. She quietly spoke with the younger, who grabbed her coat and headed out the back door. I had decided to quickly look at fabric for a new dress, and for shoes.

"There is a woman who might be able to help with your wee one," she said. "My daughter has gone to ask. Can I show you something while we wait?"

I asked about fabric for a dress.

"No, I'm afraid not," she said. "We just found the bolt end of red and white check from Fourth of July table cloths a few years ago. There is the white over there, but not even enough to make a shirt for a boy."

I said I'd take it, and a McCall's pattern to go with it. I needed to start somewhere.

"Shoes?" I asked hopefully.

"Oh, no," the woman behind the counter said regretfully. "We haven't had shoes in a good while. Even if we did, not many people could afford them at war prices."

I nodded that I understood. New shoes were more than I had expected.

"Where do you live?" the woman asked.

She seemed to have reason beyond general

nosiness. So I told her where I had settled.

"We heard that house had sold, but we didn't know to who," she said before she leaned back with a knowing smile. "I was going to tell you to be sure to sign up for your ration book. Now I can tell you that, and to look under the floorboards. That old lady hid this and that, and we never knew where. If she had something of value, we thought it might be under the floorboards."

At the moment I didn't care about something like stashed silver teaspoons. And I didn't hold much with gossip and rumors. I needed shoes.

"Thank you. I'll be sure to look around," I said noncommittally.

The younger woman returned through the back door, along with a gust of fresh air.

"She said she has to go see her sister this afternoon, but then she can go over," she said to her mother.

Smiling with the satisfaction of a venture gone right, the older woman turned to me.

"You will have some help with the baby. We know a woman who is weaning one of her own. She'll stop by here later, and we'll send her over."

I was ever so grateful, and said so.

"What should I pay her?" I asked.

"Like as not she'll want nothing," the older woman said with a flutter of her hands. "But I'll let you two work that out."

I paid for my purchases, tucked the fabric under the baby blanket, and promised to return the jars the next day. Feeling a little more optimistic, but rudely awkward in life, I set off to scald milk.

Sometimes I'm surprised any of us survived that era.

True to her word, someone did come to help feed my little boy. She said she had been looking for a good excuse to wean her youngest child. We talked over a plan as she fed my boy. She said she could come in the morning and the evening, and maybe after lunch. If she could, she would leave some milk for a feeding in the night. That seemed uncommonly generous. I told her I was eternally grateful, and asked what I could pay her for her kindness.

"I'm happy to do it. It's what we do for each other. Besides, money doesn't seem to be much good these days, even if a body has it to spend," she replied. "But I'd take some of the fruit from your orchard when it is ripe, if that's all right with you. We don't have fruit trees on our place, and my brood would take high pleasure in having some this year."

"I would be most agreeable to that," I said. "There are plenty of trees out there. I couldn't tell you what they are until they bloom."

"Oh, we all know that orchard," the woman smiled as she moved the little mouth from one breast to the other. "You have apples, pears, peaches, and cherries. Did you know there is a little cemetery back there? Gooseberries are out in the fence. You must know about the strawberry patch. Rhubarb is by the barn. And out in the timber you have walnuts and pecans."

"Well that's certainly more than I need," I said. "I'll be more than happy to share."

"You might be able to sell or trade, too," the woman told me. "Tinkers and gypsies come through here. So do traveling salesmen. It might not do to trust any of them to the end of time, but it's okay to do a little trading."

I wasn't sure I would know a tinker from a gypsy from a traveling salesman. All I knew was that none of them seemed to be held in high regard. Even so, I thanked her for the advice. I appreciated knowing my options.

Babies are a lot of work. I had no idea. At home the older children helped take care of the younger. And there was always a grandmother, aunt, neighbor, or healer woman somewhere nearby. Someone always knew what to do with a particular quirk or condition. But alone, I was always unsure and exhausted. It wasn't that I regretted the decision to keep my son, but I did question the wisdom of it. He seemed to grow and change a little bit every day. Maybe it would have been different if I had been able to feed him myself, but it was more than that. Every day there was something new to do, or think about. I felt like I was drowning.

Help did come. The woman who fed my son arrived one evening with a jar of thin soup and a hunk of cornbread wrapped in paper. She told me to eat and go to bed. She would tuck in my son after he had been fed. I was ever so grateful. From then on she offered to let me go to bed early and tuck in my son until his next feeding during the night. We would chat a little bit before I would, thankfully, go to bed.

My visits to the general store occurred almost every day. I went for milk, and to return the cleaned jars from the day before. Fresh milk was not always available. I tried draining the fluid off of cooked oats to add to what little I might have. My son did his best with it. Still, I didn't like the idea.

One day I walked through the door of the store to find the women behind the counter in a flurry of excitement. They both bent behind the counter and came up with a can in each hand.

"Tinned milk!" the older woman exclaimed.

"Condensed milk!" the younger one

corrected. "We have been trying to buy some of this for you, but it always went past us to the war effort."

My pocket held only enough to purchase one tin. That was fine. I didn't know much about milk in a can, although I'd heard of it. Once I was home, I poured the contents of the can into a pan. It was thick. Before I heated it for my boy, I added a little water.

He liked it. He drank nearly all we had, with his little hands wrapped against the bottle. Then he slept for three hours instead of two. As soon as he was awake we went back to the store for the other three cans, and I told the folks there I would be eager to know if they thought they could find more.

While my son had been asleep I took the time to write a quick letter to my friend, the minister's wife. There was so much to tell her. I told her about the house, what I thought of Missouri, so far, and where to send a letter so it would reach me. But I didn't mention my son. I don't know why. Maybe it was all still too much. Maybe I couldn't share the truth about him. I knew I couldn't lie to her.

I also wrote a letter to the chaplain the minister had told me to contact once I was settled. I thanked him for his help, and asked if he would arrange for my widow's pension check to be sent.

How long it would take to receive one, I did not know. But with some of my money stolen, I knew I would need it a little sooner than I had first thought.

When I went to the store to buy the canned milk and post the letters, I asked about shoes and lengths of fabric, as I almost always did. Still, there were none to be had.

One morning as I looked out the window above the kitchen sink, and saw the vegetable garden beginning to sprout shoots above the soil, it occurred to me that I had never been beneath the trap door in the pantry to investigate the cellar.

It turned out to be bigger than I expected. There wasn't much down there, but I always figure every little bit helps. In the light of the open door I found buckets of sand holding carrots, beets, parsnips, turnips, and rutabagas. A small store of potatoes and apples were in wooden bins along one wall. Along another were crocks of pickles and fermented cabbage.

I've never liked fermented cabbage.

I brought up close to a fourth of the vegetables in the basement. After I'd sliced them into bits and dropped them into a black iron skillet with some oil and water, I went out back to find some spring greens to include. I didn't find anything but violets and lamb's quarters but there was plenty of each.

Dandelion and plantain were along soon after. It is always such a comfort to have enough to eat.

One afternoon, after I had been looking at the tiny beginnings of fruit where the blossoms had fallen from the trees in the orchard, a young man on a bicycle rode to the front of my house. My son was inside sleeping. I walked around from the side yard to catch up to the young man before he knocked on the door. He asked my name to be sure he was at the right house.

From a leather pouch at his side, he solemnly removed a yellow envelope. It was a telegram.

For a moment I looked at the telegram in the young man's hand, remembering the last time I had seen one. As I slowly reached for it, I think I heard the young man say he was sorry. And then he was gone. No doubt he delivered a lot of bad news.

I sat on the front steps for a while before I had the courage to open the telegram. I knew the worst message had already been sent. My husband had already been killed. I slid my finger under the seal of the envelope. Maybe this one was simply a mistake.

It was from a lawyer. My mother-in-law had died. They had been looking for me, as the widow of her son. She had no will. I would inherit.

I didn't want her things, her home, or to go back. I knew that in an instant. All I wanted were my husband's belongings. I wrote a letter to the lawyer saying so.

Three weeks later a parcel arrived. The lawyers had used the same box the Army had provided for my husband's personal effects. His khaki uniforms were there, along with a photograph of him wearing his dress greens. Slowly I laid my fingers on his medals, dog tags, and identification. His childhood toys and three photographs of him as a boy were included. On the very bottom was his high school diploma and graduation photograph.

I opened the envelope that had been on top of it all. The stationary inside showed law office letterhead. The lawyer explained the house and contents had been sold to pay my mother-in-law's debts and legal expenses on her estate settlement. The envelope included a check for a small amount left over. It was enough to be helpful. I took it to the bank and opened an account.

A week after that my pension check arrived. For some reason, seeing the envelope made me cry. Maybe I was tired. Unreasonably, I felt that if I sent it back my husband could come home. Maybe it was seeing his things again. It had made me tender inside. Maybe I finally fully realized he wasn't coming back. For whatever reason, I cried.

Without my saying a word, a new story traveled around the small town. People began to regard me with kindness and care, and told me they were sorry for my loss. Some offered general assistance or prayers. Dishes of food appeared at my door in front of women offering condolences. One older woman included a black dress with a spool of matching thread. She had worn the dress while she was in mourning, she said, suggesting that I could take it in at the seams. I sincerely thanked each and every one.

I never lied. I really had lost my husband, even if it wasn't as everyone believed.

Holding a baby is comforting, no matter what. Sometimes I held my son just to make myself feel better. Looking into his little face, whether he was awake or asleep, seemed to set me right with the mysteries of the universe.

A chicken turned up in the coop one day. I asked the woman who still came to help feed my son if she knew where it might have come from. She said her family had taken some of the chickens when the house had become vacant. Different chickens had gone to others in town. Standing outside the coop, she said the chicken inside had been one of two that had escaped their yard. She told me to keep it, saying she had no use for a wandering chicken.

I asked if her family enjoyed the taste of

fermented cabbage. She said they did, and had run out late the previous year. That day she left with a gallon crock of the smelly stuff.

Now, that's a good trade.

By this time I had begun to talk with my son. It seemed to make him happy. He liked for me to make goofy faces and funny voices. Sometimes I'd hold him and talk about baby things right to his face. Sometimes I would talk to him about almost anything while I was working at something else in the room. If I had to work outside, I set him in blankets on straw in the washtub, and moved him from one shady place to another as the day wore on. I'd talk to him so he would know where I was, and that he wasn't alone. But if my thoughts turned me quiet, he didn't seem to mind. He was a good baby.

Sometimes I talked to my husband, too. It just seemed right to let him know what was going on. I don't know if he heard or not. I didn't figure it hurt anything, one way or the other.

The other chicken that had wandered off of my new friend's place eventually turned up at mine. I kept it. Between the two I had all the eggs I needed, and some to spare. It was a good thing to have enough to trade, sell, or give.

Speaking of giving, I gave the woman who had owned the chicken another crock of fermented cabbage. I think I had the better of the deal.

One day, when she had come to feed my son, I mentioned the cabin on the property. I said I had never seen it. I wanted to go there, but didn't think it wise to go alone. The Depression had displaced so many people. And criminals would hide anywhere. For all I knew, someone who didn't care for company might be living there.

She said she knew right where it was. She had played there as a girl, and wouldn't mind seeing it again. She suggested we go see it the next day, sometime after the morning dew had dried. She would bring her oldest and youngest daughters along, since the oldest had finished school and the youngest hadn't begun.

The cabin was closer than I thought. Once I knew where to look, I could see it from the house through the trees in winter. It was in better shape than I imagined, too. The roof needed patching, and some of the window glass was broken. Trees had begun to grow too close. The whole place needed a good cleaning. But the stone fireplace and chimney were as solid as ever. Sitting not far from the creek, I imagined it was a pretty place in its time.

While we were there I commented that I was pleased to see something new and different. I'd grown up in one spot, and had come to appreciate seeing new places.

"Why don't you take the train over to the

State Capitol at Jefferson City?" the older daughter asked. "There's one that goes there and another that comes back every day."

I hadn't known that. I'd heard the train, but hadn't seen the depot at an edge of town I hadn't explored.

"I want to go, but Mom won't let me go alone, and she thinks my friends are too young to go on their own, too," the oldest daughter continued. "I want to go find a job, with the war on and all."

"You're too young," her mother said sternly. "Besides, I need you at home."

Later, when her daughter was out of earshot, I asked my friend if she would mind if I took her daughter to Jefferson City.

"I wouldn't mind seeing it, and maybe your daughter would see enough to change her mind," I said. "I promise to keep her out of trouble."

Two mornings later, my son in safe in my friend's hands, I settled onto a train for the first time. It reminded me a little bit of my first time on a bus. I wasn't alone this time, either. I had company, who was so excited she wiggled in her seat and talked nearly the whole way there.

The Statehouse could be seen for miles from town. The train stopped at a station downtown, just a few blocks down a wide, brick street from that grandest building I had ever seen. Sitting on the bank of the Missouri River, the wings seemed to reach wide in either direction from under a dome that sent light everywhere. I could only imagine what went on behind the brass doors that reached up to two stories. I was sure whatever happened there must be very important.

On either side of the brick streets of downtown, shops and offices sat in tight rows. The general stores were all twice the size of the one in my new home town. I was struck by it all and barely heard the chatter of the girl next to me. We walked from one street to another until I spotted a shoe store. I had been aching for new shoes for so long. I bought some, and a pair of work boots.

At a second-hand store I bought some clothes I could wear while working outside. Among them was a pair of trousers. Women had begun to wear trousers to work. Eventually I cut down my husband's khaki pants to wear while working. There were those who disapproved, but no one could deny the practicality of it.

My companion wanted magazines, so we stopped at a bookseller. While she flipped through the racks, I walked through a section of used books. There were so many I wanted. I settled on *Gone with the Wind*. I'd heard a lot about it. And, with no more time than I had to read in a day, I figured that particular book would keep me busy for most of a year.

Then I came to a rack of bibles. It dawned on me that all families had bibles. My family had begun without one. There were so many. The shop owner saw me hesitate, and offered to help. He asked what kind of bible I wanted. I had no idea. I told him I wanted the one with the most in it. He handed one to me that had *The Apocrypha* in it. I didn't know what he meant. But I could see it was the one with the finest cover and the most pictures. I thought it must have something to do with that.

After my companion had spent all of her money on magazines, she was ready to go. We stopped at a café for lunch, where I treated her to soda, too. She was happy. And I was pleased to have the chance to practice being in charge of myself and one other at a restaurant.

As we continued to walk among the shops and offices, my companion talked of finding a job. She speculated at how she would fit in at nearly every business we passed.

After spending time with her, I agreed with her mother. She was too young. She wasn't ready for a city.

I offered to bring her back with me the next month. I knew there was more shopping to do, and things I could trade at the general stores.

She said she wouldn't have money by then.

It was the only time in the whole trip she was quiet.

I told her I wouldn't be able to pay much, but if her mother approved, she could come work for me, now and then, when her work at home was done. I really could use some help.

She perked up again, and helped me carry my packages. She liked that idea. And, really, what girl doesn't want a chance to spread her wings a little bit?

Before we were back on the bus, I'd also purchased one dress, a hat, three plain hankies, and gloves. I couldn't stand one more day of feeling any shabbier than I had to.

My tatty looks had kept me from going out as much as might be good for me. It wasn't that I was better than other folks. But as the new woman in town, and a widow at that, the way I looked and behaved were important.

On the way home, as my companion for the day chattered on about one set of folks in town to another, I became even more aware of the way people talked. I should have known. I'd encountered the sour grapevine of gossip before. I had not given much thought to my position in my new community. At first, there had been so many difficulties in the mix. But now that it was known that I was a young widow with a baby, I would have to be careful. I had more than myself to consider. My son would grow up in that town. Perhaps for his sake more than mine, it was important to be mindful of the way others viewed me. Before the train rolled back into town, I had begun to decide how to construct a family story, what reputation to cultivate, and was determined to comb my speech into the steady, lyrical, hospitable rhythm of my Missouri neighbors.

That evening I sat at the kitchen table with my new bible. Lamplight glowing on the first white pages, I wrote my name, my husband's, and the date and location of our marriage. I could write no more than the date of my husband's death, and his Army information. I didn't know where he died. Then I wrote the date and place of my son's birth.

There were no lies in that bible. If someone from my husband's hometown ever saw it, they might know it wasn't quite the full truth, since they might remember I had not been with child when I left. But as for what I wrote, there were no lies.

When my friend came to feed my son the next morning, I gave her one of the hankies I had bought the day before. I'd stayed up to embroider the initial of her first name on one corner. I wanted to thank her for doing so much for me.

Her reaction let me know she was unaccustomed to gifts. She ran her fingers across the vivid floss, amazed that I had remembered she had once said her favorite color was blue, and folded the hankie carefully before she placed it in her pocket.

As we talked over peppermint tea, I asked her about the churches in town. One was a Catholic church. I knew nothing about being Catholic, although I later learned my bible would have been fine for it. The other two churches in or near town were of no particular denomination. She had taken her children to both, and didn't see much difference between them.

Before she left, she told me it was fine for her daughter to come work for me on Saturdays. The other children were home from school those days, and could take over her oldest daughter's chores. She said she would be happy to watch my son if going to Jefferson City once a month would still work. If I took her daughter, she said, it might be a way to grow the girl into a place she was determined to go.

That girl could work. And she was very good with my boy. As young and silly as she might have been, she was a hard worker. She went straight to work washing diapers. She pulled weeds, cut and hung herbs to dry, and with each harvest helped me set food by in the pantry or cellar. Canning is hard, hot work, and I was grateful for the help. Every Saturday she went home with her pay and something from the gardens.

Every Sunday I went to church. I wore my

black dress, new shoes, hat, and gloves, and behaved respectfully. I dressed my boy in his best dress, and took a bottle to keep him quiet.

But all three times we went to one church the minister shouted so loudly my boy cried. We couldn't keep going there.

The minister at the other church was a little quieter. But his sermons were always about the sinful nature of men and women. His face was full of spite as he spoke about evils of one kind or another. He looked straight at me, one day, when he spoke of evils of the flesh. I didn't care for that. And I didn't want my son growing up hearing so much talk about sin and nothing else. So that was the end of that church, too.

I thought about the Catholic church. But I knew nothing about being Catholic. I wasn't sure I was up to the guesswork of it all. And, I thought, a person had to be born one to be one, unless they married someone who was Catholic. And even that took some effort.

I stopped going to church. But I made sure no one saw me work on Sundays, bought something at every church fundraiser, and attended community events. And when I sent letters to my friends far away, I always wrote in large script *"Rev. & Mrs."* It was the best I could do.

As much as I appreciated seeing my friend twice each day, I knew it was not easy for her. She had been ready to wean her own child when mine came along. And she had a large family to care for. She never complained. But I knew it wore on her. I had been doing my best to buy every tin of condensed milk that became available. After one particularly lucky purchase, I was able to stockpile enough in the cellar to ease the burden on my friend. I told her she need not come twice each day, unless she enjoyed the company. She said she would come in the late afternoon, before her children were home from school. I proposed that I walk to her house, but she said toting a baby was hard work, and, besides, she enjoyed being away from home for a little while each day. She said it was a breath of fresh air.

I did tote my baby to her house, though, once every month. He seemed to enjoy going. He easily fell into my friend's arms. Before I left he might quickly be comfortably asleep or giggling with one of the other children. From there, her oldest daughter and I walked to the depot to catch a train to Jefferson City.

Over the course of a year I managed to establish relationships with some of the business owners, and found a way to trade some of the goods I produced for things I needed. While nearly everyone in small towns had access to food, they didn't have as fortunate a time with dry goods and merchandise. In large cities, it was the other way around. Since I was going back and forth anyway, it seemed like a good idea to take advantage of the difference. There was still plenty to trade locally, and I still made good on my promise to share with the woman who had so very generously agreed to feed my child.

I was able to buy more of what we needed, and a radio. It was good to hear the news and listen to programs. I wasn't quite so lonesome with a radio in the kitchen.

We worked our way from spring to summer. When the strawberries were about done, the pears were ready to harvest. Two trees of pears made for plenty of canning, trading, and fresh eating. I always left some at the tops of the trees for animals and birds. It was the same for the apple trees. Apple pies went along to church socials. Of course, mine weren't the only ones.

Picking cherries gave me fits. There were so many of them. My friend offered her family to help. I'm not sure I ever had an accurate count of how many children swarmed into the orchard that day. They had such a good time in the trees. The little ones could easily move from one branch to another. Playful shrieks and laughter were everywhere. I hadn't been around so many children since I had left home to be married.

Leaving plenty in the trees for the birds, we all still had more than made us comfortable. I enjoyed the taste of cherries, but I didn't care to sit still, for hours on end, pitting them. With a baby now on the move, I didn't sit still much, anyway. I canned plenty for the winter, and let the rest go to one market or another, or my friends.

We all were harvesting and preserving vegetables at the same time. Between the last snowfall of one winter, and the first of the next, there is always more work to do than can be done. I wondered how the old woman who had lived in the house before me had managed it all. I was exhausted. And the first night I didn't have to wake to feed a baby, I thought I had died and gone to heaven.

Actually, the first thing I did was run to his crib to make sure he hadn't died and gone to heaven. I didn't take a breath until I saw him breathe.

I had taken to leaving food from one harvest or another in wooden boxes by the edge of the road. I painted "FREE" on the side of the boxes. Sometimes I heard someone in the boxes during the night. Most of the time, the food was silently taken between dark and dawn. It didn't matter to me who took it, but some of the townfolk said I oughtn't do that sort of thing because it would attract hobos.

I told them I thought it was my privilege, as a Christian with plenty, to give to anyone who might have been forced out onto the road to travel from pillar to post, as Jesus had, with no particular place to go. I said I appreciated the opportunity to act out my faith. It was clear I hadn't responded as they wished, but after putting it that way, what could they say?

So much for that reputation I was trying to cultivate.

It worked out in my favor, to a degree, though, because the next person to stop at my house was a new minister. He said he was a Methodist, and was establishing a church just outside the other end of town. He'd learned of the food boxes at the edge of my yard from some traveling men he had put to work on the new church and parsonage. He came to thank me for all the food they came for every night, and wondered if I would take payment for it.

"Absolutely not," I told him.

I said the food out there would go to waste if no one took it.

Food should never be wasted.

He went on to tell me he could use a few more workers, if I saw any who came my way. He said he was eager to have a church and house built so his wife and daughters could join him. He said his youngest daughter was about the age of my son, who had just crawled out of his dresser drawer crib and scooted across the floor.

We talked for a little while, and then he had

to go. I wished him well in every way, and asked him to tell his wife she had a ready-made friend when she arrived. When he left that evening, I sent what was left of an apple pie. I'd eaten one piece. His smile beamed as he said he could hardly wait to take such a treat back to the men at camp. He promised to return the pie pan the next day.

The next day the minister returned the pie pan, as promised. He said several men had come in during the night, so I didn't need to watch for more. He said he had more to feed than he could put to work.

I said I could use help with gathering and splitting wood, but didn't think it wise for a woman alone to have men no one knew around the house for days at a time. Then I remembered Saturdays. I would not be alone on Saturdays. Two men could come then, since I had only one ax.

The two men who came were a grandfather and grandson. I fed them, and sent them home with food to make Sunday at the camp a little easier. It became a habit. Over the next several Saturdays, they chopped down the trees that had grown too close to the cabin, cut them into stove lengths, and stacked them near the chicken coop to dry. It wasn't enough to keep the house going through the winter, but it was a good start. I'd find more.

One Saturday, they arrived with a crib for

my boy. They had taken a shine to him, and could see he had just about outgrown his dresser drawer. They were mindful of him if he crawled too near. He was an active little boy, and they liked to be around him. Although it sometimes made me sting that it wasn't my husband there to enjoy him the way those men did, I was grateful for the way they took care of him.

I was grateful to tears when they brought a crib they had made with their own two hands. They said it was nothing but scrap lumber from the church and parsonage. And they wanted to thank me for my kindness and generosity.

I told them I knew my life was bountiful compared to others. And I believed stinginess was a shameful way to live.

They laughed and said a lot of others didn't mind being stingy and shameful.

That's how I became a Methodist. Along with a handful of hobos, I was one of the first members of the new congregation.

That's also how I became the owner of a lumber business. It occurred to me that I was not the only one around who needed firewood for the winter. The men had gone to war a good while ago. A lot of women were in factories and businesses taking care of the war effort and the nation at the same time. We were spread too thin. Fencerows needed to be cleared and repaired, and wood needed to be cut for the houses between them.

My barn had once held horses and mules. It could again. The acreage held plenty of water and grass. I wondered if I had enough for mules, tack, and a wagon. Certainly there were men, however unsuitable for the military, ready to go to work. I checked my bank book, and gave it some thought.

I continued to trade at the general store in town, and to make trips to Jefferson City to shop and barter. I tried to find the little opportunities where others might not look. And I looked forward to being out of my normal spaces with the chance to buy a book, have a meal someone else cooked, and gaze at that beautiful Statehouse at the end of manicured brick streets.

My Saturday helper continued to go with me. She was becoming more comfortable with the City, and now that she was seventeen, she felt she was able to be out on her own. So when I needed some time to take care of one transaction or another, or talk over an idea with a business owner, she and I would part with a time and place to meet again.

One afternoon I couldn't find her. She wasn't where she was supposed to be. I walked all over the downtown area looking for her. I found her outside of a brick warehouse building near the old steamboat docks on the river. She was talking with an older, stylishly dressed woman who even had a feather in her hat. The woman bristled a bit when she saw me, but took no more than a step away. She began to assess me as I approached, and I knew it.

"I've found a job!" my traveling companion called. "This lady has a job for me."

"Oh?" I said, looking from my companion to the woman she had just met. "And what might that be?"

"She said I would have my days free, and spend my evenings entertaining men who come to call. She said the job pays very well," my companion excitedly explained. "She said I would only have to work for a few hours at a time, being nice to men who visit. Doesn't that sound like the perfect job?"

I didn't take my eyes off the woman in nice clothes.

"I'm sure the devil is in the details, wouldn't you agree?"

"I'm sure I don't know what you mean," she responded stiffly.

"I'm sure you do," I disagreed.

With a sniff the woman turned and walked toward the building behind her.

With a horrified look questioning why I

would ruin such a good job offer, my young companion turned to go after her prospective employer. She began to wail at me. I caught her arm and marched her toward the train station.

"You're not coming with me again until you can find your way out of stupid. As naive as I was a few years ago, I wouldn't have fallen for that one," I fumed. "I don't know if your mother failed to have a talk with you, or if you failed to listen. But if she can't talk some sense into you, I'll give it a try myself. We're not going through that again."

She refused to talk to me all the way home. If she meant for me to be upset by that, she misread a situation for at least the second time that day.

We missed the train. We almost missed the last bus, which slowly wandered across the counties between there and home, stopping at nearly every little town along the way. We arrived well after dark.

When I picked up my son, I talked with my traveling companion's mother. I explained our tardiness, and why her daughter wore such a solid pout. The older woman's eyes grew wide and her mouth fell open as she turned a horrified stare to her daughter. It seemed like a good time for me to go home. I carried my sleeping baby along the dark streets, careful to not turn my ankle in a hole.

The next day my friend apologized about her daughter, and thanked me for keeping her out of trouble. From the look of her, she hadn't had much sleep the night before. She said she realized her daughter would never have any more sense than a chicken, and worried about her place in life. It would be a sorry thing for her daughter to live in the City, like she wanted to.

Maybe so. Not everyone was meant for a city. I pointed out her daughter was a hard worker, noticed what went on around her in familiar environments, and knew how to take care of children and a household. She wasn't feeble or lazy. I thought she would be fine if she settled into life in a place closer to home. And, I said, when she married she would have a husband to watch out for her. She might make a good small-town wife, with time in the City for fun with her husband. That wouldn't be so bad.

By the time my friend went home that evening, I think she felt better. I sent her home with all the peas and beans I had picked that day. No doubt her oldest daughter found herself busy shelling and snapping for hours.

All summer long I worked from before sunrise to after sunset. I was ever so grateful that my son had begun to sleep through most nights. Plenty of women didn't have it so easy.

When people asked about my son, I was always careful with my words. I didn't want to lie. If someone asked about his daddy, I answered about my husband. If someone asked if my boy favored his father, I said I was sure he did, at least a little bit. It wasn't a lie. I'd met the woman who bore him and knew quite well how she looked. No one would have known if I lied. Even to protect my son, I still didn't like to tell a lie. But I would, if that's what it took.

To my way of thinking, I wasn't just raising a little boy. I was cultivating a man. For him to do well in life, he needed a solid stand for himself. The way he thought of himself mattered. As for the way others regarded him, I wanted nothing to stand in the way of his own actions and achievements.

No one would have thought badly of me for raising another woman's child. But there were those who would treat my son differently if they knew he was base born to people they didn't know. It would be part of what made him. And he would grow up wondering what was so bad about him that his own mother hadn't wanted him. His father was a mystery and his mother had run off and left him.

No, we couldn't have that.

He was much better off growing up wanted as the son of a mother who clearly loved him, and a man who died a hero for his country. That story would stand him well in life.

In a way, maybe I lied. But I didn't tell a lie. I just let people think a lie. I let them believe what they pieced together without me setting them straight. It wasn't altogether honest, but it wasn't an outright lie.

In late summer, I discovered I wasn't the only one keeping secrets by keeping silent. With school out for the summer, I was able to hire some of my friend's other children to take on some of the work around my place. That way, I was able to go out for more trading and scouting. My friend's oldest son was able to come a few days to help split and stack wood. When I took out a jar of cool ginger mint water I praised his work and commented that his father must appreciate his help around their place. He stopped still and looked at me in a way that let me know I was surely missing something.

It occurred to me that I had never seen my friend's husband. She spoke of him, but never in the immediate sense. I had assumed he was always away working, or in bed asleep the one time I was there late. As I thought of the house and contents I'd seen while visiting, I realized that in all the belongings scattered in the busy place, I did not recall one thing I could say for sure belonged to her husband.

So one day I simply asked about him.

My friend sighed and looked to the ground before she answered.

"Five years ago last month he left to look for work," she said. "He hasn't been back but once for a couple of weeks. He doesn't even know about our youngest."

I hardly knew what to say. A lot of men left home during the Depression to find work. Some stayed in touch and sent money if they didn't return. Some just seemed to disappear.

"You don't hear from him?" I asked.

"He can't read or write," my friend replied.

We both knew it wasn't too difficult in five years to find someone who could write a letter home for him. I didn't press her into telling me he wasn't sending money, either. I knew she was struggling to cover the necessities of her family. A lot of people were. But I didn't realize her husband did none of the providing. She had never said a word. My heart broke a little bit for her that day.

Her husband never did come back.

Her oldest son had been taking odd jobs, but had found no steady employment locally. The military was always calling for men. Pretty soon the war might be his only option, and I didn't want for my friend to stand to lose both a husband and a son. He needed a job that made him vital to the war effort from home. I would have to think about that.

There were no factories in the area, and no businesses in need of employees. People were pretty much on their own. So I thought about what I had to work with on my place. I had a barn, an old cabin, fruit and nut trees, two chickens, and gardens. I was holding my own and keeping a few others out of the poor house, but I wasn't able to take on much more.

My thoughts returned to the barn, which was mostly empty, and the need for fence repairs and maintenance, and firewood. The grandfather and grandson who had been coming first on Saturdays and then on other days when my friend's children were there to work, listened to a few ideas and were willing to explore options. Since they had been traveling around the region, they knew more about what might be available not too far away.

Before long we had a good mule, fairly new tack, and a wagon in need of reasonable repair. We found saws here and there, a few of which had been in the barn without our ever seeing them. I wrote little cards and bought advertising in the little town paper saying the men were available for fence clearing and repair, tree cutting, and would cut and stack firewood. They could also do some light hauling.

And so they wouldn't have to go sleep in a tent with the other new Methodists every night, we cleaned and repaired the cabin in the woods behind my place. It was common for workers to live in company housing. There was no good reason to let a cabin fall to ruin when there were people ready to live and work in it. The two of them were good at clearing and building fences, and chopping wood. They had a head for business, too. They knew how to trade well. That's how I came up with three more chickens and a rooster.

But that didn't take care of my friend's son. My friend never asked me for a job for her son, but I wanted to do something to keep him near her. So when I was next in Jefferson City, I began to ask around.

It took a while, but I finally found a sawmill that had shut down during the Depression. It was between a river and a railroad spur between our little town and Jefferson City. The owner was an old man who had lost his sons, one way or another, to the war. He had no interest in the mill, but would guide someone else in bringing it back into operation, and teach a few men how to make a business of it. He knew how to come up with timber. He said he knew where to sell lumber. He had a list of customers who were still asking to place orders.

I asked him to be there full-time for a month, and then half-time for a month after that, and then as needed for advice for the rest of a year. He said he could do that. But first he wanted to meet the men I planned to put to work. That sounded reasonable. Before I left that day, I asked his price for the mill and his wisdom. When he told me I had no idea if it was fair or not, but I knew I had it. I just had it.

I spoke with my friend and her son. They were willing to give the mill a chance. None of us really knew how it would go, but other than me, no one had much to lose.

The Methodist minister was able to recommend a few men from his camp who were honest, steady workers. He said they worked well together. So I took them, my friend's son, and went back to the mill to talk with the owner. Nearly all the money I had in the bank went with us.

The mill owner and the men with me talked easily and seemed to do well with each other. The mill owner said he was willing to go forward with the plan. But when I extended my hand to shake his, he didn't move. He said there was a problem.

"I can't see myself working for no woman," he said. "I'm too old to start that kind of truck now."

I didn't know how to take that. So I asked him how many men he saw, cash in hand, ready to buy his mill.

He turned to look at the men I'd brought, who did nothing more than look back at him. So he said he'd sell, but he didn't want me around.

I didn't care for that. So I told him I had other businesses to operate, and would be able to come no more than once every two weeks, at most and in the beginning, to make sure my employees were behaving themselves.

It was then I realized we had not come to terms with the amount of land that went with the mill. He started by saying I was buying the mill and no ground. I knew I wanted land around the mill. We haggled. Eventually I told him we had come to the line I would not cross.

He hesitated. I thought his next move was to shake my hand, but he was reaching for the money.

I said I'd give it to him at the title office.

That night I barely slept. My thoughts ran wild and my stomach followed right behind. I'd just spent all the money I'd worked so hard to save. Looking back, I was downright terrified. It probably didn't help that just before bed I read the part of *Gone with the Wind* where Scarlett O'Hara becomes an outcast for owning a lumber business. But with her, there was more to it than that.

One of the front rooms in my house became an office. After my son was in bed for the night, I sat at the secretary to recorded income and expenses, keep track of bills, and to write correspondence. Sometimes I was up very late.

At first I couldn't even come up with full wages every week. The men understood. Men who have been down on their luck know when someone is sincerely trying to do something good with them. I made sure everyone was fed, and had what they needed most. They probably had their fears about the mill, too.

I was still terrified. But I'd set a course and was determined. Sometimes all anyone can do is hold on and try to not slide backwards.

My son went with me everywhere, except on the train to Jefferson City. He was becoming heavy to carry around. I began to struggle with the weight of him over a distance.

One of the new Methodists found a little red Radio Flyer wagon. It was slightly dented and a little bit rusty in spots, but clean. He said it was a thank-you gift for all the food I had supplied. And now that the church and parsonage were built, and he had a little money in his pocket, he was going home to his family. He said he hadn't seen them since late winter, and had been aching to go home. He just hadn't wanted to go home empty-handed.

There was space in his poke and I asked if he would like to fill it with some food for his journey. We found bread, vegetables, and some eggs just finished soaking in waterglass. I offered to give him the capped bottle I had used on the bus as I traveled to my new home.

He accepted, and thanked me kindly.

Not long after that I did find a treasure under the floorboards. When I dressed for a church social one Sunday afternoon I found myself chasing a button that fell off my dress. Pushing the bed aside, I crawled around on my hands and knees, certain it must have fallen through a crack in the floorboards. As I searched the edges of the boards I found one tiny spot that faintly looked like it had been repeatedly pried up and set back into place. With a spoon handle, I loosened and raised one edge. Under the board was a box made to fit under that one plank. Inside I found my button, and stack after stack of letters, each wrapped in pink ribbon and tied with a bow. The letters were addressed to the woman who lived in the house before me.

Pulling up the stack nearest me, I slipped the top letter from under the ribbon. Opening the linen weave envelope, I could see pages beautifully scripted in the Palmer method. Unfolding faintly scented stationary, I began reading. It was a love letter.

Forgetting about my button or church, I read a small amount of news, followed by tender words of comfort, heartfelt dedication, and wishes for a life of daily togetherness. My eyes filled with tears at the sight of such longing. My heart nearly broke at the unknown injustice that had kept these two lovers apart.

At the end of the last page I understood. The letter was signed by a woman.

I folded the letter, noticing the Jefferson City return address and restored it to its place under the pink ribbon. As I set the precious bundle back in the box beneath the floor, I caught sight of a gold chain on top of the next bundle. Lifting the chain revealed a gold locket. Inside were degraded photographs of two women. It seemed a fair guess they were the two lovers. My heart ached even more for them.

Maybe I didn't have a clue what it was like to be in love with another woman. But I sure knew about losing someone I loved. I wondered if the woman who wrote the letters even knew what had happened to the woman who used to live in my house. I wondered if she was worried about her letters.

Two days later I took the train to Jefferson City. I wore my Sunday best. Wrapped in an embroidered dresser scarf, the letters were in a basket next to me, under a big bouquet of cut flowers. I pushed them aside to check the envelopes beneath as I moved along the brick streets leading away from the depot. Before long I was at the matching address. I was glad to have found it, because there had been no one along the way to ask.

I hesitated on the walk outside. What would I say? I'd been thinking and rehearsing all along the way, but now that I was outside the door, I wasn't sure how to begin.

I knocked. The rap was softened by my glove. I took it off and tried again.

When the door opened I was still speechless. I found myself in front of an elderly woman with dark, warm eyes in skin near the color of home-grown honey, under hair that had once been black. I found myself thinking that the lady who had lived in my house was still full of surprises.

I'm not sure how many times the woman in the doorway kindly asked me what she could do for me before I managed to ask if hers was the name on the envelopes. It was. I stammered, at first, explaining that I lived in the house her close friend used to own.

"Used to?" she asked. "Did she move elsewhere?"

I could see the hope on her face, against the underlying knowing her loved one must be gone. As gently as I could, I said her friend had passed on, and the family had sold the house to me. I told her I was also a widow, and had made the house into a home for my little boy and me.

"I knew she must be gone," the lady in the doorway said. "When my letters came back, and I didn't hear more from her, I knew."

"Ma'am, it's the letters that brought me here," I said, pushing aside the flowers and dresser scarf so she could see the bundles in pink ribbon. "I thought you should have them. The locket is in there, too."

Shocked and flustered, the woman asked me if I would like to come inside. It seemed like the proper thing for me to do. So I did.

Her house was tidy as could be. Not one thing seemed out of place. Everything was clean, polished, and there were crocheted doilies everywhere. I barely wanted to move for fear of wrinkling something.

"These are for you," I said, handing the basket to her.

Reaching into the basket, she thoughtfully stroked the envelopes and ribbons below. As tears began to pool in her eyes, I offered to go.

"Please stay, if you can," she asked. "If you think it would be fitting."

I sat on the couch while she poured lemonade in the kitchen. It felt awkward, so I went to the kitchen doorway.

"If you like, we could sit in here," I said. "It might be more comfortable to talk at the kitchen table. It always is for me."

She set a tray of lemonade in glasses and a pitcher on the table between us. It was clear much was on her mind.

"I haven't told anyone about the letters," I offered. "I read only one to see what they were, and where they might be returned."

The woman who sat across from me seemed relieved, but she didn't seem comfortable.

"I know what it's like to be widowed," I explained. "And I know what it's like to keep secrets for the sake of loved ones. My secret may not be like yours, but I understand enough to respect it."

"Thank you," the woman at the table said as her shoulders softened. "My daughter doesn't know. My neighbors don't know. We fell in love after my husband died while my daughter was still a little girl."

"Yours was a long love," I said.

"It was," she agreed. "It was an impossible love. We did as well as we could with it, but it never felt like enough. It's difficult for something so bright to live in the dark."

I could only imagine. Of all the difficulties I had weathered, hers was nowhere near anything I had to face. Everything about them had to be hidden.

"Would there be more hidden under the floorboards in that house?" I asked.

"No doubt there is," the woman across from

me softly smiled and reached to the basket on the table. "Where did you find these?"

Once I told her, she ran down a list of other places under the floors, in the closet under the stairs, and false bottoms of dresser drawers. She said there might even be a few "articles of interest" behind the dresser mirror.

Assuring her I would return what I found, I said I would check around as I could. From the sound of things, I wasn't sure I could find it all quickly.

Saying I had some business to conduct in the City before I had to leave on the train, I stood to go. I promised to return.

A thought struck as I left the house. I turned back to the woman standing in the doorway.

"Do you have any idea where the keys to that house might be?" I asked. "I've never been able to find them."

She smiled at me. It was easy to see memories passing through her mind.

"The key to the front door hangs against the inside leg of the secretary. It's on a nail way up at the top near the back of the bottom drawer," she said. "The key to the back door is on top of the porcelain lid of a canning jar, under a rock beside the pansies at the edge of the back porch. It was there for me to use as I could. I think there is another one hanging behind the wood box for the kitchen stove. I only ever saw the one kept outside."

Sure enough, she was right. The keys were where she said they would be.

The next few weeks, during rains when my son was napping or asleep for the night, once my paperwork was done I set about finding all those hiding places. There were more letters tied in pink ribbon, pressed flowers in books of poetry, penciled bookmarks that would have easily fit into a mailing envelope, and a few photographs. One showed the pair of them smiling in a joyful embrace. On the back someone had penciled *Paris 1926*.

The last hiding place I found was under the bottom shelf in the cabinet under the stairs. Had I not known to look, I'm sure I never would have. There I found a metal box holding travel brochures and a stash of currency and coins. They had been saving for another trip to France. Had it not been for the war, they might have been able to go.

The next month I returned to Jefferson City with another basket of letters, books, and photographs, the metal box. As before, it was wrapped and covered with a large bouquet of cut flowers. This time I included a jar of fresh strawberries. It was a heavy basket.

When I reached the porch of my new

acquaintance, I set down the basket and knocked at the door. She didn't answer. A younger woman did. She politely greeted me. I asked if it was a good time to pay a call.

The young woman introduced herself as the daughter of the woman I had come to see. She said she wouldn't be ready for visitors for a couple of hours, but I was welcome early, if I didn't mind that the food hadn't been set out yet. She stepped back so I could come inside.

I was about to explain that I didn't want to intrude on any plans, and that I had brought some things I could drop off without interfering, when I saw the casket in the corner of the front room. I realized my new acquaintance had passed.

"I'm so sorry," I said. "I didn't know. I'm sincerely sorry for your loss."

"I'm not sure how far word has spread. I'm still making arrangements," her daughter said. "Did you know her from the College?"

"The College?" I asked.

"Lincoln College," the daughter explained. "She used to teach the domestic arts there."

"Oh. No. I wish I had," I said, knowing I could have used that sort of guidance. "I met your mother last month. I brought some property of hers to return. I live in the house where her good friend...traveling companion...used to live. She passed a while ago. I found more, and thought your mother might like to have it."

Walking to the coffin, the daughter looked at her mother in the coffin for a moment before she turned to me again.

"Letters?" she asked.

"Yes," I said carefully. "And some photographs, with a few other things."

"Keep them. I really don't want them," she said. "I found my mother in her bed. Open letters and pink ribbons had been scattered across the covers. She died under them. It was as if she knew she was going, and wanted those words with her. Maybe she wanted to go. I read enough to understand. But I don't want to read any more. I didn't know."

"I'm sorry. I don't know much about it, either," I said before I proceeded cautiously. "All I really understand is how much and how long they cared for each other."

"I didn't know," she repeated, seeming to not know what else to say.

"I don't want to intrude on your grief," I said, standing as I reached for the basket. "Oh, I just remembered. You might want--."

"No," the woman in front of me said. "No,

thank you. There really isn't more that I would want."

I nodded, taking my hand from the inside of the basket. To push would have been to disrespect her grief. I stepped out onto the porch, and expressed my appreciation for having had the chance to meet the woman in the coffin before she died. It was then a thought came to mind.

"You mentioned all arrangements had not yet been made. I would like to extend an offer for you to consider," I began. "Your mother's companion is at rest in a small family cemetery behind the orchard on the property that is now mine. The space next to her is available. It would be my honor if you would consider laying your mother to rest there. I understand you might want for her to be buried next to your father."

"My father is buried in Louisiana," she said. "Thank you for your offer. I'd like a little time to think, if you don't mind."

I assured her I understood. I told her which train I would be taking later, and said I would arrive a little early to look for her. Then I asked her if she would at least take the jar of strawberries. I didn't want to carry any more weight around Jefferson City than I had to.

She was waiting when I arrived at the depot. She agreed to her mother joining her companion in the orchard cemetery, provided that the burial was conducted in private. She said she would have preferred a minister's presence. She didn't think it would be easy to arrange.

The Methodist minister agreed to come, but quietly. We all agreed; the fewer questions to answer, the better.

Someday I hope such matters can be conducted differently.

Every day was busy from before sunrise to after sunset. But I made sure no one saw me work on Sunday. Often I caught up on bookwork that day. And I began to notice the numbers didn't seem quite right at the sawmill.

I talked to my friend's son. He said the former owner of the mill was the one to deal with sellers and buyers, and always insisted on being alone. There seemed to be some unusual exchanges, in my friend's son's view, but he couldn't be sure.

I took the time to check. With my ledger and invoices in hand, I went to talk with the owners of the businesses involved. After comparing entries, we realized many of the dealings between businesses had been tainted by greased palms and kickbacks.

"This is why we stopped dealing with that mill a while ago," one business owner told me. "It's also why his sons want nothing to do with the business. We thought a new owner might do business by the light of day. We didn't know the old guy came with it."

Of all the things I did and didn't know, I was sure reputation was everything. I made sure that man knew we did do business by the light of day, and that the 'old guy' would be gone the moment I arrived back at the mill.

"He's been cheating us both," I said. "Make sure everyone knows that man is no longer part of the operation, and I take pride in fair dealing."

We shook hands, and I left. As I walked away from that particular lumber yard, I wondered if Scarlett O'Hara shook hands with her customers.

On the way out of town I stopped at the sheriff's office. I said I was about to fire someone who had been stealing, and I didn't think he was going to take it well. I would appreciate it, I said, if a lawman could be there to maintain the peace, and be sure the understanding of trespassing was clear. He asked who I was referring to. When I told him he said he would be happy to come along, so long as I understood that such stealing was a civil matter. He couldn't make an arrest until a judge issued a warrant.

That old miller would have made a fuss if the sheriff hadn't come with me. As it was, he demanded that I pay him before he left. I told him I was sure he had stolen more from me than I would have paid him through the terms of our agreement, and suggested we call it even. I also said if he ever showed his face on the property, he would be trespassing. He started to fuss and cuss and holler at me when the sheriff stepped in and said something to the old coot about the cots in the jail being no more comfortable than the last time he was there.

That was the end of it. I appreciated that sheriff.

My friend's son was the only one of the men who worked there who was interested in organizing and supervising any of the work. Being an oldest son of a missing father and a steady, hard-working mother, I figured he would do fine. The other men, having been wandering, knew of new businesses to try to sell lumber, and land in need of clearing. In time the Methodist camp closed, and most of the men went to work at the mill. We built a bunkhouse on the road beside the mill. I told the men they could live there as long as they worked at the mill. But if they wanted a wife, they were on their own.

Speaking of wives, the Methodist minister's wife arrived. She told me it was the first time she had been in a house that smelled so new. She was excited about her new home. But I think being back with her husband had a lot to do with her outlook. We were both pretty busy around the time she arrived. But later, when the season took a turn, we had a little more time to become better friends.

Church was open. The minister was ready for whoever came on Sundays. I made sure my son and I were there, and at all the appropriate events in between. We had lunch outside at first, and in the back of the church when cold weather arrived. We became extended family, in a way, and talked of adding on to the church.

We all met for a huge Thanksgiving dinner in my barn. It was a good excuse to clean the barn from top to bottom. We set up one big table made of planks on sawhorses. Food came with nearly everyone who arrived. It was such fun.

By the time the winter solstice arrived, the gardens had been put to bed, making for much less outdoor work. Potatoes and garlic were in the ground and covered with a thick layer of straw to begin growing as winter allowed. There were the chickens, an additional mule, and the donkey that came with it. The owner said he couldn't feed the donkey in winter. And, besides, he said, the two of them had been together for years, and he didn't want to separate them.

It was a good thing the two men in the cabin out back had also traded for more hay and feed than we thought we might need in winter. There is no telling what might happen.

Donkeys and roosters are good about protecting their home. I thought they would be worth their keep for that alone. They raise a ruckus when something isn't right.

They raised a bit of a fuss when an old, overloaded wagon came down the road one morning. But I heard it, anyway, with the merchandise clanging against the sides. It was an old man and woman behind two horses who appeared to be almost as old. I felt for them all.

They asked if I would be interested in buying or trading. Honestly, I was. Gift-giving season was approaching, and I had little to offer. I told them they could rest their horses while we traded. There was water under the windmill and feed in the barn. They were welcome to a couple of flakes of hay, and some grain.

When the grandfather and his grandson heard the noise from the wagon, they came to trade, too, and amiably brought the grain and hay. A little bit of molasses had been stirred into the grain.

Those were some very happy horses.

The couple spoke with an accent I couldn't place. I didn't want to be rude by asking where they were from. We could understand each other very well, and did a lot of trading. I found a lot of what I could give as holiday gifts. Along with a little cash, I traded away the red and white check fabric I couldn't seem to use, the blue and black buttons I had salvaged from dresses, apples, root vegetables, grain, and a few more flakes of hay.

I heard my boy up from his nap and went inside while the two men traded for what they wanted. By the time I was back outside they were finished, and were hitching the horses to the wagon again. The old couple exclaimed something I didn't understand when they saw my son. They fussed over him a bit as they prepared to go. They said they were on their way to meet their daughter and her husband who also had a little boy. They were anxious to see him.

The two old traders seemed happier when they left. Maybe it was my son who brought those smiles to their faces. Maybe it was all the trading we did. I'm sure the horses were happier, too, because we certainly lightened their load.

As nice as those two old people were, I kept an eye out, just the same. I'd heard such traveling folk might circle back to a place and steal. I was determined to be alert to the sound of unwanted visitors, particularly at night. But all was quiet. I was glad, because I liked those old folks. They would be welcome if they came back.

In a short while the acreage and the mill both became profitable, but not by much. Knots in my stomach and racing thoughts in my head kept me awake in the night. I had to admit I had never been taught about money or business. I thought things through and asked those I trusted for advice. When something didn't go right, I backed up, looked it over, and gave it a try again. Sometimes I walked away. I tried to calm myself by saying no one could do more than her best, and that's what I was doing.

My friend's son came to the house one Saturday and told me he needed to join the war. It was a surprise, particularly since his mother and I had worked so hard to keep him home. He explained he was grateful for the job, and hoped it would be there for him when he returned. It was the return from war that had been on his mind. Among the men in town his age, he would be one of the very few who had not served his country as they had.

It was then I realized I had been thinking like a mother. His mother was a friend. We were determined to keep him safe from war.

But as a man, he needed to go to war. To not go would make him different, and maybe less than other men his age. It would shape the rest of his life.

So I said I understood, and told him a job would be waiting when he returned. A burden seemed to lift from his shoulders. It occurred to me that he must have been thinking about that conversation for a long time.

The bank foreclosed on the property next to mine, which had been, along with my acreage, part of the original homestead. It was for sale. When I had the money to buy a few acres of it, I asked the man in charge of loans at the bank if they would be willing to sell that much.

He said they wanted to sell the land as a whole parcel, not break it up. He offered me a mortgage. When I declined, he told me a mortgage would make life easier, and that I could own all the property at once. He wasn't very happy when I asked him how a mortgage on the land made life easier for the people who owned it before the foreclosure. He said I didn't understand mortgages.

I was pretty sure I did.

Keeping a solid roof over my son's head and good food in his stomach was first on my mind. I was determined to make sure I stood on solid ground. Other than a family, I was never prepared for much responsibility. Now a lot of families depended on me.

By spring my son was walking. It amazed me how slowly we walked down the road, with me holding his hand, but as soon as I let loose of him and turned my head, he was off like a shot and into something before I knew it. I found him by following whatever commotion he created. I think he explored the world by crashing into it, one way or another.

But the real worry was when he was quiet. Then I knew he was somewhere or into something likely to cause trouble. I never knew where I would find him.

One summer he went through a spell of throwing off his clothes and running wild around the yard, and a few other places. He hates it when I tell that story.

In town one day I found my son with a dog. It was a half-starved thing with sad eyes and gentle ways. From then on out we had a dog living with us. He was a loyal dog, who kept a close eye on my son and the rest of the place. He was of undiscernible heritage, like most Americans. He fit right in.

Everybody carried on as best they could until the war ended. All of a sudden everything felt different. We knew the Depression wasn't coming back. But we didn't know what was ahead. The men began to trickle home. So did the women. Without a war, there was no place for women in factories and offices where the men wanted to return to work. Ships were slow moving men back home. A lot of women did their best to hold onto their jobs. We lived with a new kind of uncertainty. I just did what I had to do with every day in front of me.

One thing was sure, though, was the demand for lumber began to take off. The Government was helping men from the war come home to home ownership, and a lot of building was going on all over the country. While we had long daylight in summer, we were able to run two shifts at the sawmill.

I bought more wooded land to clear. And I bought scrub and spent land to plant trees. Eventually I bought back much of the original homestead, with cash.

I never did learn to trust a mortgage.

My friend's youngest children, along with the Methodist minister's children, earned money planting trees. The littlest earned a few pennies for dropping acorns, walnuts, or pecans into holes an older child had dug. My friend, the minister's wife, and I made banks out of jars with coin slots pounded into the lid for each child. Even my little boy toddled around with a pocket full of nuts to plant, and later dropped pennies into his own jar just as happily as the bigger children.

There's nothing wrong with teaching little ones about work and money.

One morning, almost at the same time, the dog, rooster, and donkey raised the alarm that something was wrong. I went out to find a man up on the back porch. The dog had him fairly cornered at one end, while my son held tight to my husband's childhood toys at the other.

After praising the dog, I called him off, pointing for him to go be near my son. He did.

"It's a good thing he minded you," the man told me. "A dog like that, I might have had to break his back."

I was shocked. I was offended. I was angry.

"I heard about you, Little Missy," he continued, looking around my place. "You got all this land and business that needs tending. That's bound to be more than you can handle, particularly being a widow with a little child and all."

This arrogant man was making my blood boil as he strutted around the yard and gardens. He kicked at the corner of the porch after he had circled back. He looked me over in a way that made me very uncomfortable.

"So I thought I'd come over and check it out," he said, blatantly eyeing me. "Check you out."

When he finished scanning me up and down, he looked at my son in a way that made me ready to fight.

"I don't see anything here I couldn't handle. I'd be willing to take you on, you and your brat. He'd have to know his place once my own children come along, you know what I mean? I always wanted an untried woman for myself. But a man's got to give a gal some leeway, and do his patriotic duty for the men who died by taking on what's left behind. I'd do you that favor."

That was more than I could take. Out of the corner of my eye I saw my son's eyes grow wide as I exploded into the most unladylike language that has ever come out of my mouth. In no uncertain terms I told that sorry specimen what he could do with the bit of anatomy he intended to aim at me, along with the rest of what he so prided about himself. Somewhere in the streak of blue air I fired at him I made it perfectly clear that if he ever so much as aimed an eyeball at me, my place, or anyone or anything on it, that I would shoot his sorry ass and bury him under a pile of manure where he belonged.

In a rage, he man charged me. My son screamed. The dog lunged. I picked up an axe handle leaning near the pile of firewood on the porch. The dog had him first, but I did my part. When I called the dog away it was a sloppy mess that headed for the road, threatening all sorts of unpleasantness when he returned.

That man scared me. And I didn't really have a gun.

I closed the dog and my son in his bedroom and ran across the fields to town to buy whatever firearm was available. Nearly breathless, I explained at the general store what had happened. The man behind the counter gave me the rifle he thought most fit me, and a box of cartridges. When he asked if I knew how to shoot, I told him every girl who grew up where I did knew how to handle guns. As I began to run for home, the store owner called to me that he would inform the sheriff.

Everything was fine when I arrived back at my little farm. I loaded my rifle. The sheriff came. I barely slept for a week. But I never saw that sorry so-and-so again.

Late that summer, on the train home from Jefferson City, I met someone. He was coming home from the war, judging by the uniform he was wearing. The train was rather crowded that day, and I asked him if I could take the seat next to him. He smiled and rose so I could have his seat by the window. I knew there was something different about him as soon as I looked into those clear, honest, compelling eyes.

Or, maybe it was something different about me. Inside I felt a flip when he looked at me.

Whatever it was, he had my attention. And I had his. We talked all the way home.

He was just home from the war, and planned to begin law school at the University of Missouri. He was on his way to visit his sister until the semester began. She was the Methodist minister's wife.

When I told him about me and my little boy, he let out a cheer and a laugh. His sister had written about us in letters to him. He said he felt like he knew me already.

I wish I could have said the same about him. His sister mentioned she had a brother in the military, but didn't say much more. She could be very quiet.

Her brother wasn't. He and I had no trouble talking. That was the shortest train ride ever. I could hardly believe it when they called our stop. There seemed to be so much more to say by the time we had to leave the train.

He found me, though. He walked over nearly every day. He helped out around the place. Sometimes I saw him in town or at his sister's house. We did a lot of talking. We did a lot of smiling and laughing, too. Even my boy joined in. I was pleased to see the two of them take to each other. Sometimes they took off without me so I could have a little time alone. If nothing else, on Saturdays they went to the store together for penny candy.

I missed that man when he left for law school. He took the train to visit his sister on holidays, semester breaks, and for the summers. I looked forward to his visits to his sister. When he left to go back to Columbia, I always asked when he thought he might be back. Before long we all knew he wasn't coming so often to visit just his sister.

He stayed with his sister to work during the summers, but not for me. He found something to do at the courthouse in town. I never really knew what he did, but he sure looked handsome in a suit.

My friend's son returned from the war and went back to work at the sawmill. Before long I could rely on him to run everything. I rarely had to be around. We met over what had to be done to maintain the business in good standing. That meant equipment upgrades and buying a couple of trucks.

I insisted on learning to operate the equipment and drive the trucks. What if war broke out somewhere and took the men away again? It seemed like a good idea to be prepared. There were folks who didn't approve of a woman knowing such things. But I was sure Scarlett O'Hara would have done the same thing if trucks had been around in her day.

One winter evening I found myself facing a pretty new ring and a proposal of marriage. His sister said it took him long enough. He waited until the last semester of law school. By then he had given the matter a lot of thought. He said he would come to town to join the one attorney there. And he would be agreeable to living in my house, provided we installed electricity beyond the one wire in the kitchen, and indoor plumbing.

I had no trouble agreeing to that. The man gave me the tingles when he looked at me, and I don't think it had anything to do with electrical wires or water pipes. Besides, my boy was at an age when he needed a man to guide him the way only men can do. He needed a father.

I thought long and hard about telling my fiancé about the lie on my son's birth certificate. For months I struggled with the uncomfortable notion of beginning marriage with a secret in the mix. He was a good man and I adored the way he was with my son. I didn't think the lie would matter to him.

But what if I was wrong? What if one day, for even a second, it did matter? What if they locked horns as men do when the younger one reaches an age of independence? Would anger reveal the lie in a hurtful way that could never be taken back? That kind of damage could never be undone. How would my son feel about himself? How would he feel about me for keeping such a secret from him for his entire life?

I looked at that birth certificate many times as I pondered the possibilities. In the end, the evening before the wedding, I folded the lie, tucked it in the back of my dresser drawer, and never mentioned it.

There were two people in the world who knew the lie. For years I was worried the other would come back to take my son, but I never saw or heard from her again. After this long, I didn't think I ever would. My son would never have cause to think he was less than anyone else in this world.

So now, as I am a grandmother, widowed again, watching my son's children playing with him in the yard, I think about the lie. Should I tell my son? I am old. There may be few opportunities to reveal the truth, if it matters.

Does it matter?

No. It doesn't.

The truth is that no matter how this young man came to be mine, I am his mother. That is the truth, even if it began with a lie. I will say nothing.

Truth is often what we make of a lie. And what we leave behind matters. I'll let the truth live on when I join the others in the little cemetery behind the orchard.

What I'll take with me will be the lie.

Elizabeth Rowan Keith is an award-winning author and artist. She is a researcher and professor of sociology, cultural geography, ethnobotany, government, and American Indian studies. She is the widow of author David H. Keith, and presently lives in Saint Louis Park, Minnesota, where she practices as a healer and communicator.

Made in the USA
San Bernardino, CA
21 December 2017